<u>Rich</u>

<u>A Vanguard Origin</u>

<u>Written By:</u>

R.D. Wolfe

Table of Contents

Chapter I – The Child Famer

Rich pressed the spade into the earth, hoping for weight. The soil collapsed—light, dry, another loss. He crouched, his larger than average frame casting light shadows on the ground. Brushing the top layer aside dust rose around him, dry and bitter on his tongue. Beneath it, the earth wasn't much better.

The soil along the edge of their area of the valley looked promising from a distance—rich and dark with the early-season frost melting back—but Rich knew better the moment he pushed his spade in. What looked like humus was just dustbound sand with a layer of rotted leaf mold. It would hold for shallow roots, maybe turnips or bitterrad, but the west rows he'd planned for beans would have to go somewhere else. Too loose, too dry, and no time to rebuild the rows from scratch. Not with the stronghold's move clock already ticking.

He stood upright and stretched his back, the wool lining of his coat sticking to his neck where sweat had already begun to gather. The cold air bit at the exposed skin between glove cuff and sleeve, but he didn't adjust. The labor demanded motion, and motion beat warmth.

To his left, Mita was threading new pipe. Her hands were pink with the pre-dawn chill, fingers stiff as she fumbled with the feed cap.

"You're past the notch," he said without looking.

"I'm not."

"You are." He stepped closer and tapped the coupling. "It's off by a hand. You'll bleed runoff into the low beds."

Mita narrowed her eyes but reseated the joint with a heavy twist, driving the rubber collar flush to the marker groove. She was twelve. Old enough to argue, but still young enough to be forced to listen when she didn't want to.

They worked without further conversation. Rich turned and knelt into the loam, laying compost mulch along the irrigation trench as the filtered lines began to thrum. Along the edge of the field thin trexium cables pulsed faintly, drawing from the portable grid installed by the outpost's engineers just days before. The relay hub blinked near the edge of the field—soft pink light behind a reinforced lens—marking out one of a dozen agricultural blocks feeding this stronghold during its tenure in this new valley.

Rich struggled with new valleys. The idea of something new was appealing. New soil, new views, new land. Even new crops were tried from time to time if the season turn was right, which it usually wasn't. What he didn't like though, was ripping out months of work. Spending the time growing the food to feed his neighbors and diligently molding the earth to his purpose, only to have to scrub it away. He would erase the fact that he had labored with such diligence; they all would, and then they would move.

This would hopefully be a full four-month cycle. A hundred and ten days, give or take, before they'd pack the trexium cores, disassemble the walls, and haul the stronghold to its next site. Rich didn't waste time wondering where that would be, or what the new challenge would be in this valley. He had enough to worry about in the dirt beneath his feet.

They were lucky to be coalition. Not outsiders. Not fringe farmers clinging to independence or rogue settlers trying to make their own rules. Among all the farmers, he was moderately happy with their plot. Their spot outside the walls had been drawn by the planning officers three nights before setup, and Rich had been present when the boundary was staked. He remembered standing there, arms crossed as the engineer drove the corner post into the frost-hardened ground and asked for a name to enter on the records.

"Rich Halden," he'd said, not hesitating, even though the words tasted foreign. The pad had chirped, and the quartermaster nodded like it was nothing.

"You got anyone else with you?"

He had pointed behind him. "Mita. Hagan. They're listed."

"Parents?" Then man asked, seeing the youth in Rich's intentionally impassive expression.

He shook his head. The man was smart enough not to ask the follow up question. Perhaps it was the size of Rich. He was at least a full head above the man, even if he was likely twenty years Rich's elder.

The quartermaster had scrolled through the old data block anyway, verifying the connection. "Says your parents were listed on the prior site?"

"They were. They're not here now," Rich replied flatly, leaving very little room for interpretation.

The man made a note, signed off, and passed Rich the field allotment band.

His parents' names were still in the system, but now they only existed in the archived logs. Inactive. On current records, Rich would carry the custodial mark. He was now the one assigned to submit crop counts, report energy draw, and show up for headcounts. No pity, no compassion. Just a nod and a line on a tablet. That was what was given to him by the people he kept full.

His mind came back to the present as he paused to check the pulser box beside the feed hub. The casing was scraped but clean. No condensation inside the lens, and the conduits still held a charge. The engineers had warned him about current fluctuations in the first week. New lines always ran hot or cold depending on load variance, and they were drawing more than their share with early crop heat.

From the roadbed that traced the base of the southern ridge, the stronghold's upper gantries came into view. Four towers, boxy and functional, with rotating spotters and directional panels. Light shimmered once from a moving patrol. Just enough to catch the corner of his eye and ground him.

He, Mita, and Hagan, broke for rations when the sun crested above the ridgeline. The food was simple—pressed root cake, flatbread, a strip of dried apple with crystal salt. They ate sitting on overturned crates, the scent of compost and frost-thawed earth strong in the still air. Mita kicked her boots together to keep circulation up, or maybe just to have something to do. Hagan tore his bread into triangles before eating it, like always. Routine kept them steady. Rich leaned against a supply barrel, arms crossed, eyes on the trexium relay blinking across the row.

A high voice echoed from the northern fence line.

"Your goats are out again!"

Rich rose, brushing grit from his knees. Two pale shapes darted along the fence margin, tails high, hooves churning soft mud. The older of the goats had found the slope break again—where the wire didn't reach the ground cleanly over the shale.

"I'll go," Rich called.

"No, me!" Hagan came bounding down the rise, his jacket undone and a length of feed twine slung over one shoulder.

Rich let him run. The boy needed the movement. Instead, he decided to check the perimeter. Make sure there weren't other issues in their newly built little farm plot.

He took the long route along the perimeter, checking post seams as he walked. The frost hadn't lifted in the shade, and the moss grew thick under the trees. The slope narrowed where the southern irrigation ditch ran alongside the wall of the miner's corridor—low, grooved dirt that heavy carts passed through on their way to the nearby claim. From where Rich stood, he could hear the deep mechanical thrum of the diggers pulsing beneath the surface. It was a different sound than the relay hum—lower, like something breathing just under the earth.

He paused beside a tree line where the ditch curved. A pair of trexium haulers rumbled through the shallow pass below—no escort, just two rigs and a signal flare stowed behind the last crate stack. Both drivers wore reinforced sleeves with coalition arm markings, though the vehicles bore the dull grime of field equipment. No shine. No ornament. Just iron and function.

He remembered Mita asking him once, squatting beside a broken reel of conduit while they waited on parts from the supply lines. "Where does all the trexium go after they dig it up?"

Rich had shrugged. "Powers the walls. The lights. Our tools."

"Yeah, but after that," she'd said, scrunching her nose. "There's so much of it. Doesn't it go anywhere else?"

He hadn't known what to say. There were always haulers. Always crates. Always movement. But where it all ended up—he couldn't picture it. He just knew it wasn't here.

That conversation came back to him now as he watched the rigs bounce over the pass. Someone else moved it. Someone else turned the pink glow into the hum behind their heat and the pulse beneath their feet. His job was just to make sure they didn't go hungry doing it.

He crouched in the shadow of a brush cluster and watched as the haulers reached the inner fence and were waved through by two soldiers at the south gate. Their rifles stayed lowered, but their eyes tracked the path behind the rigs long after they passed.

Rich stayed there a few moments longer. Long enough to see one of the guards murmur something into a shoulder mic and glance uphill. Rich stood slowly, and resumed his route back toward the clearing.

When he returned, Hagan was leading one goat by the neck while the other followed, bleating indignantly. Mita stood beside the cookhouse door, checking a reading on the heater gauge. She looked up when Rich approached and smiled—not the wide grin she used to flash when their parents were still with them, but the tired kind that meant she saw him and still trusted things were okay. As okay as they could be, anyway.

That night they ate stew over flame, the broth salty and thick with greens. The goats were penned. The children laughed. Mita repeated a joke Rich had told days earlier and made it funnier in the telling. Hagan fell asleep halfway through chewing, head tipped against Rich's shoulder.

They weren't just children. They were his siblings—his to feed, to shelter, to raise. Since the accident last move, since the breach at their last... home was the wrong word. Either way, it had been Rich who handled the ration cards and signed the logs. Who lied to the quartermaster when he needed to and gave up his own plate when the numbers didn't stretch. Coalition records still listed them as dependents. At least that part was still true.

They slept just beyond the stronghold wall. They had a makeshift house that they set up and tore down with every cycle. It wasn't much, but it was home.

Rich lay still a long time, listening to their breathing, steady and slow in the dark. Tomorrow would be more of the same. Up before sunrise, hands in the dirt, growing food to keep the Coalition running.

"Keep the stronghold strong, son."

That's what his father has always said. He had taken pride in their work. Rich did too, but his job had gotten so much more complicated since...

Rich shrugged the memory off as he began searching for sleep. The thrum of the pink energy source beyond the walls acting as a buffer between him and the silence that let his mind wander. He counted the waves of noise.

One... two... three... four...

Sleep finally found him just as the memory of his mother's smile and the warmth of his father's strong embrace carried over into troubled dreams of his last memory of them alive and the torture that awaited him in their ethereal presence.

Chapter 2 – The Ones Who Watch

The morning came early, as it always did for Rich, pressing cold air through the small gaps in the shutters before the sun had even touched the ridgeline. He rose quietly, careful not to wake Mita and Hagan, who lay curled tightly beneath a shared blanket, their breathing synchronized in the deep rhythm of sleep. Outside, frost shimmered softly over the fields, outlining the neat rows of crops in a thin, brittle silver.

He dressed quickly, pulling his heavy coat over layers worn thin from use, slipping his gloves into a pocket rather than putting them on just yet. The chill woke him, sharpened his senses, and cleared away the lingering edges of sleep. The day's tasks were already forming a neat list in his mind—irrigation checks, boundary repairs, supply inventory—but his first act was always simpler, quieter. He stood for a moment at the door, glancing back toward the sleeping forms of his siblings, allowing himself the brief comfort of knowing they were safe. Then he stepped out into the cold dawn.

The soil crunched underfoot, the frost barely thick enough to hold his weight before crumbling softly beneath each step. Rich knelt by the irrigation lines, his breath forming small clouds in the air as he carefully inspected the couplings. The pulsing hum of trexium energy vibrated gently beneath his fingers, confirming the cables were stable and intact and using the strange pink energy to draw the water along its current. He adjusted one coupling slightly, careful to align it precisely to ensure the water would flow evenly when the midday warmth softened the frost.

The sound of quiet footsteps broke his concentration, followed by a stifled, high pitched yawn. Rich didn't look up. He already knew who was there.

"You're early today," he said softly, adjusting another valve.

Mita knelt beside him, pulling her coat tighter around her small frame. "Couldn't sleep anymore. Thought I'd come help you."

Rich glanced at her briefly, noting the stubborn set of her jaw, so reminiscent of their mother. He didn't smile outwardly but felt the gentle tug of affection pulling at his heartstrings. He took in her expression for a moment, but quickly tried to hide his reaction.

"Check the eastern row for runoff," he instructed gently, his voice low and steady. "The frost looks thicker there."

She nodded, rising quickly and moving toward the task with the brisk efficiency she'd learned from their parents. Watching her, Rich felt a pang—not quite sadness, not quite pride—more an acknowledgment of the world that had forced her into maturity far sooner than was fair. It had done that for him too, but he hadn't ever thought about it in relation to Mita or Hagan before. Now he had no choice but to think about it.

From behind him, another voice called loudly, somehow already fully roused from sleep. "Wait for me!" Hagan emerged from the doorway, struggling to pull his boots on as he stumbled toward them.

Rich shook his head gently, exhaling a slow breath that caught briefly in his throat. "You could've stayed inside a bit longer," he said, masking his concern with practicality. "It's early."

Hagan straightened defiantly, his eyes wide with the stubborn pride of someone determined to prove himself useful. "I can help too," he insisted, his voice soft but unwavering.

Rich paused, studying his brother carefully. The determination in Hagan's face was unmistakable, his jaw set much like Mita's, but the innocence there was still preserved in a way that Rich found himself fiercely protective of. He relented with a gentle nod, motioning toward a stack of supply crates. "Help me inventory the spare couplings," he instructed. "Make sure the seals aren't brittle."

Hagan brightened immediately, moving swiftly toward the crates as if they'd been hiding a secret reward. Rich watched him, a faint, almost involuntary smile briefly touching his lips before disappearing again. He straightened slowly, stretching the muscles in his back, eyes instinctively scanning the perimeter and then drifting further outward, beyond the clearly defined boundary of their stronghold. His gaze lingered on the distant rise of hills, where sparse trees marked the edge of their secured territory. Beyond that, it was more strongholds, more groups of people who formed coalitions and between here and there... Rich tried not to worry about it.

As he started to bring his gaze back to the task at hand, a subtle shift of movement caught his eye—just a flicker, a shadow standing slightly apart from the dark line of the trees. It was too far to discern detail clearly, but Rich could see that whoever it was stood completely still, framed between two bare, twisted trunks, watching silently. A quiet, insistent discomfort settled into Rich's chest. He narrowed his eyes, trying to pick out any familiar detail—coalition clothing, a familiar shape—but found nothing reassuring.

Then, as quickly and quietly as it had appeared, the figure stepped back into the thicker cover of the trees, vanishing from view. The spot where it had stood was once again empty, leaving only a vague unease that lingered persistently in Rich's mind.

"Rich?" Mita's voice, tinged with concern, broke through his quiet reverie. "Everything okay?"

He turned slowly, forcing his expression into calm neutrality, not wanting his tension to transfer to her. "Just thinking," he replied softly, his voice even and controlled. "Keep an eye on the eastern row. Make sure it warms evenly."

Mita hesitated for a moment, her sharp eyes reading more than he intended to show. Then, with a quiet nod, she resumed her work, her movements precise, her small frame silhouetted clearly against the slowly rising sun.

Rich watched her a moment longer, feeling the quiet weight of his responsibility settle more heavily upon his shoulders. Then, with careful, deliberate motions, he returned to his tasks, his attention sharpened by the subtle but persistent sense that they were not alone.

The sun had risen enough to burn away most of the morning frost, leaving the soil damp and dark beneath Rich's boots as he walked toward the stronghold's inner market. The area bustled gently with activity—quiet negotiations, friendly bartering for small handmade treasures and goods. Rich had always found the market intriguing; everyone within the coalition had enough food, water, and shelter, the basic assurances of survival. But it was the small luxuries, traded carefully and thoughtfully, that reminded them of being human—bracelets woven late at night by tired fingers, specialty clothing sewn carefully by lamplight, art painstakingly etched into bits of reclaimed wood or polished stone, each piece representing precious time stolen from the relentless demands of survival.

Rich carried a small bundle of dried medicinal roots they'd carefully harvested from a small corner of their fields, one reserved explicitly for trading purposes. They were valuable, offering health and comfort beyond basic survival, a commodity always in demand. It felt odd sometimes to offer such precious items just for a small taste of sweetness for his siblings or perhaps a rare bit of fabric. Yet Rich had learned early the profound value these seemingly small comforts could provide.

At the market's edge stood the supply depot where Ana worked, carefully organizing goods and engaging in patient conversation with each person who approached. Her dark hair caught briefly in the sunlight as she turned, her expression warm, eyes thoughtful and attentive. Rich felt his breath catch slightly, a quiet appreciation lingering in his chest. Ana noticed him immediately, her smile deepening as he approached.

"Rich," she greeted him warmly, setting aside a carefully folded bundle of hand-woven cloth. "It's good to see you. How are Mita and Hagan?"

"Doing well," he replied quietly, placing the small bundle of medicinal roots onto the worn wooden counter. "They're growing faster than I can keep up."

Ana laughed softly, genuine warmth in the sound. She carefully picked up the roots, inspecting them closely with practiced hands. "You've dried these beautifully," she said appreciatively. "These will help many people. They're valuable—more so than most realize."

Rich nodded slightly, acknowledging her words with quiet humility. "Glad they can help."

Ana glanced up at him, her eyes thoughtful. "So, what are you looking for today?"

"Extra seed, if anyone has surplus," Rich replied carefully. "We've got plenty for the regular planting—the coalition's taken good care of that—but I was hoping to try cultivating a small surplus. Something we could trade next cycle."

She nodded knowingly. Seed distribution was carefully managed by coalition leaders, essential to keep everyone fed and the stronghold stable. Every farmer, including Rich, was critical; without people like him producing more than they could consume, the coalition itself would collapse. Rich felt the weight of that responsibility daily, understanding too well that his ability to cultivate even a small surplus meant others might find enough time to craft something beautiful, something comforting—something human.

Not to mention the soldiers and the vanguard, who fought to keep their walls safe. Without people like Rich, they would run out of steam. The trexium miners wouldn't have the strength to keep digging to keep the fields humming with power. Everyone counted on food. And it was his job, among others, to grow more than he needed to feed everyone else.

Ana turned toward a neatly organized shelf, pulling down small cloth bundles labeled with carefully sewn letters. "I think I can help," she said thoughtfully, selecting two small packets. "Leora from the farms in the second section had extra ryegrass and cabbage seeds. She came through this morning, mentioned she'd trade for medicinal roots if you stopped by."

Rich felt quiet gratitude toward Ana for having anticipated his need, for quietly looking out for him. He nodded, carefully accepting the seed packets. "This is perfect. Please tell Leora we appreciate this."

Ana smiled softly, her expression gentle. "You're easy to barter for, Rich. People know how much you do for all of us. If your fields thrive, we all thrive. It's the most essential trade we make."

Rich felt his cheeks warm slightly at the quiet praise, unused to acknowledgment of his efforts. He glanced down briefly, slightly awkward. "It's just our part," he said softly. "Everyone does theirs."

Ana tilted her head slightly, considering him gently. "True enough," she conceded warmly. "But it's not lost on anyone that your part lets us do ours. There's no art or comfort without food. You're giving everyone else the chance to be something more than survivors."

Rich was silent a moment, absorbing her words deeply. They reminded him of the importance of their endless toil—not just for survival, but for those brief moments where life held meaning beyond the next meal. Finally, he spoke quietly, sincerely. "Thank you, Ana."

She shook her head gently, her eyes soft. "No need to thank me. Just keep bringing medicinal roots, and I'll keep finding ways to help you."

Rich hesitated briefly, then glanced down at the carefully wrapped seeds. "Maybe a little dried fruit, too?" he asked quietly, his tone gently hopeful. "Hagan's been asking."

Ana laughed again, warm and genuine, already reaching into another crate. She pulled out a small bundle of carefully dried berries, handing them over gently. "Tell him not to eat them all at once this time."

Rich allowed himself a small smile. "I'll try," he replied, knowing full well the chances of Hagan following such instructions were slim at best.

Their fingers brushed briefly as he took the bundle, sending a small, pleasant jolt through his chest. Ana's expression softened slightly, a quiet warmth passing between them. "I'll see you again soon?" she asked, a gentle hopefulness in her tone.

Rich nodded quietly, his voice gentle but firm. "You will."

As he walked slowly away from the market, he held onto that warmth, carefully protecting it as he stepped back into the harsher reality that awaited him beyond the gentle, fleeting comfort of Ana's presence.

When Rich returned home, the sun had begun its slow descent toward the western ridge, casting long, slanted shadows across the fields. The carefully wrapped seed packets and dried berries were tucked safely beneath his coat. He felt cautiously hopeful, buoyed by Ana's gentle warmth and quiet generosity, even as he navigated the familiar paths home.

But as he approached their plot, something caught his eye—a slight irregularity. The gate latch was partially undone, swinging gently in the breeze. His steps slowed instinctively, senses sharpened, every small detail suddenly meaningful. He carefully inspected the latch, noting the fresh scrape marks against the metal. He couldn't recall having left it unsecured. A brief but intense unease tightened within his chest.

Rich checked the perimeter swiftly, his movements deliberate yet cautious, finding no further disturbances. Still, a quiet anxiety that he couldn't shake continued to linger. He discreetly reinforced several of the gate fastenings, tightening bolts and checking hinges without drawing attention to himself. The task calmed him marginally, yet the unsettled feeling didn't vanish entirely.

He stepped inside as the fading sunlight painted the walls amber. Mita stood by the stove, stirring a pot with careful focus. She looked up and smiled, eyes bright. Hagan sat at the table, braiding lengths of twine into a small bracelet, his concentration joyful.

"What took you so long?" Mita asked lightly. "Hagan's been eyeing the door."

Hagan grinned sheepishly. "I wasn't worried," he protested.

Rich managed a small smile, producing the bundle of dried fruit. "A surprise," he said.

Hagan's eyes widened. "Ana again? I told you she likes you."

Mita giggled softly. "He's right. You smile more after visiting the market."

Rich felt warmth rise slightly in his cheeks. "She's just kind," he murmured. "Eat the fruit slowly, Hagan. Don't finish it all tonight."

Hagan nodded seriously, the mischievous gleam in his eyes suggesting he'd already disregarded the instruction.

They ate together, the stew simple and nourishing, filled with familiar comfort. As the night wore on and the fellowship of family took hold, Rich found himself forgetting about the gate and the unease that settled on him at its being open. At least for tonight.

Chapter 3 – The Empty Spaces

The morning came quietly, softer than usual, as if even the valley itself sensed something was different. Rich stepped outside early, feeling the cool air brushing gently against his face, carrying the scent of ripening fields. Almost two cycles had passed since his last visit to the market, and now, with harvest season approaching, their small plot was flourishing. He allowed himself a slow breath, letting the calm of the early hour settle into him. For a brief moment, the heavy sense of responsibility felt lighter, softened perhaps by the promise of a good harvest and the quiet anticipation of seeing Ana again.

He moved through his chores with practiced efficiency, carefully checking the robust growth of their herbs and crops, ensuring each plant had enough water and support to withstand the coming weeks. Over the past month, he'd spent long hours cultivating the medicinal herbs, knowing they'd trade well at the market, not to mention give him the excuse to travel into the stronghold market again.

Mita and Hagan emerged from their sleeping quarters just as Rich was finishing, yawning and stretching lazily in the warmth of mid-morning sun.

"You could have woken us up!" Mita said chidingly.

"You needed to sleep. You need all the rest you can get before harvest day. It's not far off. Besides, there wasn't much to do." Rich replied, concealing the fact that really, he had just been enjoying the quiet without the burden of care taking that kept him so busy these days.

Mita eyed the bundle he had tucked under his arm.

"Going to trade again today?" Mita asked, her voice still thick with sleep, though her eyes sparkled knowingly. "Seems like it's been a while."

Hagan grinned openly, nudging Rich playfully. "Make sure you tell Ana we said hello. It's been ages."

Rich felt warmth creeping up the back of his neck, but this time, he met their teasing with an easy smile. "I'll be sure to do that," he replied lightly, resecuring the carefully wrapped bundles of herbs. "Maybe I'll even bring you two back something nice."

Mita raised an eyebrow mischievously. "Just don't stay out too late," she teased gently. "I'll try to keep Hagan from waiting by the door all day."

"I don't do that!" Hagan protested

"Oh yes you do," Mita countered back, annoying Hagan in only the way that siblings knew how to.

"Nuh uh!"

"Sure Hagan, keep telling yourself that." Mita replied finally, letting the conversation fall away as she saw the youngest of them becoming red in the face.

Rich shook his head, chuckling softly as he continued working, setting the children on their chores through the day, waiting until early late afternoon when the market would open for business once people were done with their days work.

"You two be good, try not to annoy each other to death, okay?" Rich chided, half amused.

"When are you gonna be back?" Hagan asked.

"Not sure, will depend on what I find, but if I'm not back before bed just make sure you brush your teeth."

Hagan scowled. Getting him to brush his teeth was usually a twenty-minute ordeal.

"Please Hagan? Just tonight, make it easy on your sister if I'm not back?"

"Ugh, fine."

"Don't worry, I'll take care of it," Mita said confidently, filling the role of the matriarch of the home a little more each day.

Rich smiled and hugged them both before turning and walking out of the gate he had spent time working on earlier that season. He thought back to the night that he had last gone to market and found it open. There had been nothing since then to indicate any trespassers. That had eased his mind, though it had taken an easy two weeks to settle.

Rich approached the stronghold gates just as the late afternoon sun touched the tip of a mountain on the valley edge, casting long shadows over the imposing entrance. The gates themselves were massive, built from reclaimed metal and reinforced timber, weathered and scarred by years of movement and use but still sturdy and imposing. Two coalition guards stood vigilantly at either side, their expressions neutral but watchful, eyes scanning each person as they passed through.

He nodded briefly to the guards as he stepped past them, receiving brief nods of acknowledgment in return. Inside, the stronghold bustled with carefully controlled activity—Vanguard soldiers moved purposefully through the crowd, their distinctive armor gleaming subtly under the sun, the soft pink glow of trexium cores visible in the weapons strapped to their backs. Their presence was both comforting and unsettling; a constant reminder of the dangers that lay beyond these walls.

Nearby, a group of trexium miners trudged slowly toward the residential quarters, their faces and clothes streaked with pale dust, exhaustion evident in every step. Rich caught fragments of their quiet conversations, words heavy with fatigue and cautious optimism about the day's yield. Their labor was critical—every harvested trexium shard a lifeline for the stronghold's survival, powering everything from irrigation systems to perimeter defenses.

The market itself hummed with vibrant life by the time Rich arrived, its energy contagious and comforting in its familiarity. Stalls lined the pathways, each carefully assembled from salvaged wood and sturdy canvas, showcasing meticulously crafted goods and freshly harvested produce. The air was rich with the mingled aromas of fresh bread, pungent herbs, and faintly sweet dried fruits, all combining into a scent uniquely associated with market days.

Rich navigated through the bustling crowd with practiced ease, exchanging quiet nods and brief, friendly greetings with fellow coalition members. Many faces were familiar, their expressions ranging from the careful optimism of those whose harvests promised abundance to the quiet resignation of those who knew they would have to barter carefully for extras to carry them through leaner weeks.

As he approached Ana's stall, Rich felt an involuntary lift in his chest, the anticipation pushing aside the lingering worries that so often shadowed his thoughts. Ana stood behind her counter, gracefully arranging vibrant bolts of fabric dyed in earthy shades and carefully packed bundles of dried herbs. Her movements were precise yet gentle, each gesture imbued with care. Sunlight filtered softly through gaps in the stall's canopy, illuminating her dark hair in warm, coppery tones. When she glanced up and caught sight of him, her eyes brightened immediately, drawing a genuine smile from Rich.

"Rich," she greeted warmly, placing a neatly wrapped parcel gently on the counter. "I was starting to wonder if you'd make it today."

Rich returned her smile, carefully setting his bundles of medicinal herbs down between them. "Harvest is getting close," he explained softly. "It took a little longer than expected to gather enough worth trading."

Ana carefully lifted one of the bundles, her fingers brushing gently over the fabric wrapping. Her expression grew thoughtful as she inspected each bundle in turn, her eyes filled with quiet admiration. "These are perfect," she said softly, glancing up at him warmly. "You always put so much care into your work, Rich. It shows."

Rich felt a flush of warmth spread across his cheeks, unused to such open praise. "I figured you'd put them to good use," he replied gently, his voice tinged with modesty. "Maybe trade for something special, for Mita and Hagan."

Ana's smile deepened, her gaze softening with quiet appreciation. "Actually," she began hesitantly, leaning slightly forward as if sharing a gentle secret, "a few of us are gathering tonight—nothing big, just some food, a bit of music. It might be good for you to step away, relax for a while. I'd like it if you could join us."

Rich hesitated, immediately torn between his ever-present responsibilities at home and the rare chance for respite. He glanced briefly toward the busy market around them, his thoughts momentarily drifting to the myriad tasks still awaiting him. Yet when his eyes returned to Ana, her quiet hopefulness held his attention, gentle yet undeniably persuasive. Plus, Mita had already said she'd take care of Hagan's evening routine, and dinner was already pre-prepared.

Finally, he offered a slow, genuine nod. "Alright," he said quietly, his voice holding a quiet determination. "I'll come."

Her eyes lit up instantly, the warmth in her smile chasing away any lingering doubt. "I'm glad," she said softly, sincerity evident in every word. "It'll be good for you, I promise. I'll see you tonight?"

Rich nodded again, the weight on his shoulders feeling lighter than it had in weeks. As he stepped back into the bustling market, Ana's words lingered warmly in his thoughts, carrying a promise of simple joy he hadn't allowed himself in far too long. The anticipation of the evening ahead gently eased the familiar, constant tension in his chest, giving him a quiet strength he hadn't known he'd been missing.

Rich wandered through the market for a short while longer, taking in the lively atmosphere, savoring the rare sense of ease that accompanied his acceptance of Ana's invitation. With some time left before evening fell, he found himself drifting toward the dining hall, a communal space bustling with quiet, purposeful activity.

The dining hall was simple but well-organized, lined with long, sturdy tables built from reclaimed materials, polished smooth from years of use. At the serving counter, coalition workers distributed meals with practiced efficiency, their movements swift and precise as they portioned out carefully rationed servings.

Rich accepted his plate gratefully—a modest helping of stew, thick with root vegetables and chunks of dried meat, accompanied by dense, grainy bread. The rations were modest, reflecting the final stretch before the harvest brought new abundance, but the aromas were comforting and familiar, promising warmth and nourishment.

He took a seat at the edge of a table, quietly savoring the first few bites. The flavors were simple, familiar, and satisfying, carrying with them a sense of reassurance that came from knowing the scarcity of this period was almost at an end. Around him, miners, farmers, and craftsmen ate in companionable silence or engaged in subdued conversations, their voices blending softly into a background hum.

As Rich ate, his thoughts drifted again to Ana and the evening ahead. The anticipation added a subtle sweetness to each bite, enhancing the modest meal. It had been a long time since he'd allowed himself such a simple pleasure, and he found himself quietly grateful for the chance, brief though it might be.

Finishing his meal, Rich rose from the table feeling more content than he had in weeks, his steps lightened as he moved toward the gathering Ana had promised. Tonight, at least for a short while, the burden of responsibility felt distant, softened by the warmth of the simple comforts he'd allowed himself.

The evening gathering was modest, set in a quiet corner of the stronghold reserved for communal events, nestled beneath gently flickering lanterns that cast a soft, golden glow. Rich paused briefly as he approached, taking in the carefully arranged space, the warm, inviting atmosphere so different from his daily life of constant vigilance.

Small groups of coalition members clustered around sturdy wooden tables, each table holding plates of simple, nourishing food and cups filled with a mildly sweet tea, warmed by the lanterns' light. The hum of quiet conversation mingled with occasional bursts of soft laughter, creating a comforting background that felt both unfamiliar and deeply welcome to Rich.

Ana spotted him first, her face lighting up immediately, drawing his attention away from the room itself. She stepped away from her companions and moved toward him, her movements graceful and unhurried. "You made it," she said warmly, her voice soft yet filled with genuine pleasure.

Rich offered a shy smile in return, his shoulders relaxing slightly at the warmth of her greeting. "I promised I would," he replied quietly, allowing himself to meet her eyes fully, feeling an unexpected ease settle over him.

She guided him gently toward a group seated near the musicians, introducing him with quiet pride. Rich exchanged greetings, shaking hands and nodding politely, warmed by the easy welcome he received. Ana stayed near, her presence reassuring, her easy conversation filling moments when Rich found himself uncertain or shy.

As the musicians began to play, Rich found himself drawn into the soothing melodies—simple, heartfelt tunes played on handcrafted instruments of carved wood and taut strings. The music was gentle, yet carried a depth of emotion that seemed to capture the quiet resilience of their community.

Throughout the evening, Ana's attention never fully strayed from him. They shared quiet conversations about the upcoming harvest, the small moments of daily life, and gentle jokes about trivial matters. Occasionally, Ana's hand brushed lightly against his arm as she spoke, sending subtle warmth through him and making him momentarily forget his usual reserve.

Hours passed gently, the atmosphere becoming warmer and more relaxed as people shared stories and memories, laughter coming more easily and voices becoming softer, closer. Rich found himself wishing the night could stretch on indefinitely, that he could hold on to this rare, simple pleasure forever.

Eventually, as the lanterns dimmed slightly and some coalition members began to quietly excuse themselves, Ana stood with Rich at the edge of the communal area. Her expression was gentle; her eyes filled with quiet affection and sincerity. "I'm glad you came," she said softly, her voice tender. "I really hope you'll come again."

Rich hesitated briefly, his heart and mind both pulling at him. The realities of his responsibilities awaited just beyond the circle of lantern-light, yet here, in this gentle moment, those burdens seemed distant, manageable. "I'd like that," he finally replied, his voice quiet but certain. "Thank you for tonight."

Ana smiled warmly, her gaze lingering gently on his face. "Take care, Rich," she whispered softly, her words carrying both affection and quiet understanding.

As Rich began the slow walk back toward his home, he felt the evening's warmth still surrounding him. He moved unhurriedly, carrying the memory of Ana's smile and the comforting sounds of music and conversation. The reality waiting for him at home would return soon enough, he knew, but tonight, at least for a short while longer, he allowed himself to savor the gentle, rare peace of the evening he had spent.

As Rich neared the farm, the tranquility from the gathering lingered gently around him, easing his steps. Approaching the gate, he noticed Mita's scarf tangled loosely in the fence, fluttering softly in the evening breeze. He paused briefly, a faint smile touching his lips as he picked it up, assuming she'd dropped it while playing or perhaps helping with the evening chores.

The gate itself was slightly ajar, creaking gently as he pushed it open. Rich felt a brief flicker of annoyance at the oversight, making a mental note to remind Hagan once again about keeping it secured. The yard was quiet, and he stepped carefully along the path, noticing the porch light still burning softly, casting warm amber circles onto the ground. Another oversight, he thought mildly, switching it off with practiced ease as he moved past.

Entering the house, he immediately noticed the subtle disarray—nothing alarming, just slightly out of place. The chairs at the table weren't pushed in neatly; a cup of tea sat untouched, long cold. Rich shook his head slightly, smiling softly to himself at his siblings' carelessness. He quietly moved around the small living area, straightening objects almost absentmindedly as he went.

In the kitchen, Rich paused again, noticing a knife resting at the edge of the counter, its tip coated faintly in dirt. He frowned briefly, puzzled, but placed it carefully back in its proper drawer, thinking Hagan must have used it to help gather herbs or cut twine.

The silence felt oddly heavy, and Rich glanced toward the sleeping quarters, seeing that the curtain was drawn back slightly, revealing a sliver of darkness beyond. He hesitated for just a moment, an unexplainable unease gently brushing against him. He moved softly toward their room, peering inside.

The beds were empty, blankets tossed haphazardly aside, pillows lying at odd angles. Still, nothing seemed immediately alarming. It wasn't unusual for Mita and Hagan to fall asleep in the common area when Rich was out late.

Yet, a subtle discomfort tugged persistently at him, nudging him back toward the main room. He stepped carefully, quietly calling their names, his voice low and gentle at first. Receiving no response, he raised it slightly, a quiet edge of uncertainty entering his tone. "Mita? Hagan?"

Only silence answered him, the kind of silence that seemed to hold its breath alongside him. Rich felt his pulse quicken slightly, anxiety beginning to twist in his chest. His eyes moved carefully around the room again, this time noting smaller details—a knocked-over chair, a few scuff marks on the floor near the door, a small tear in the corner of the window curtain that hadn't been there before.

His breathing grew shallower as he pieced together the subtle disturbances, each small detail suddenly heavy with sinister meaning. Rich moved swiftly to the porch, scanning the darkness urgently, the scarf in his hand now feeling impossibly heavy. A cold realization settled sharply into his chest, stealing the air from his lungs.

Mita and Hagan were gone.

Chapter 4 — Into the Wolves' Den

Rich stood still for a long, tense moment, Mita's scarf clenched tightly in his fist, heartbeat pounding fiercely in his ears. Then, instinct and urgency took over, propelling him forward. He moved swiftly but methodically around their small home, his eyes sharply scanning every inch of ground, every shadowed corner.

Outside, under the pale moonlight, small disturbances in the soil caught his attention immediately. There were faint footprints, lighter and smaller—likely Mita's—accompanied by deeper, heavier impressions. His chest tightened as he followed the marks carefully, his steps quiet but increasingly urgent.

He paused at the fence line, noticing broken twigs scattered across the ground, snapped and bent away from their usual neatness. He knelt briefly, fingertips brushing over the disturbed soil, feeling the depth of the tracks. Something else—a small scrap of cloth caught in a thorny branch—was just visible in the dim light. Rich carefully freed it, heart sinking as he recognized the familiar fabric of Hagan's shirt.

"Mita! Hagan!" he called, his voice firm but controlled, carrying a faint edge of desperation that he refused to let overwhelm him. He strained to listen, holding his breath, but heard only the quiet rustle of wind through the trees and his own uneven breathing.

Moving further out, Rich spotted another faint sign—a patch of flattened grass and scattered stones—indicating a brief struggle. His breathing grew tighter, his chest heavy with dread. His mind flickered to the figure he had seen in the trees before. He knew now with grim certainty that his siblings had not simply wandered off; they had been taken.

Rich straightened slowly, his mind racing as he glanced back toward the distant lights of the stronghold, feeling a surge of determination mixing with cold, focused anger. He would find them, no matter what it took.

Rich turned sharply, his heart hammering so fiercely he felt dizzy. He broke into a jog, feet pounding along the familiar path toward the stronghold, each breath ragged in his chest. The distant lights grew brighter, reassuring at first, but quickly losing their promise as a sickening doubt twisted inside him.

He reached the towering gates, chest heaving, eyes wide and desperate. The guards straightened abruptly, their casual chatter fading away at the raw panic etched across Rich's face.

"My siblings," he gasped, struggling to steady his voice. "They're gone—taken. I found Hagan's shirt torn by our fence. Someone took them."

The nearest guard, an older man with a deeply lined face, raised a calming hand, his expression shifting into practiced neutrality. "Take a breath, son. Kids wander off all the time. Could they be playing a game or—"

"No," Rich interrupted sharply, his voice cracking under the strain. He thrust Hagan's torn shirt toward the guard, his hand trembling visibly. "They wouldn't. There were footprints, heavy ones—someone else's. Please, they're in trouble."

Another guard moved closer, cautious but serious. His eyes met Rich's briefly, then flickered away uncomfortably. "We'll file a report. Patrols go out first thing—"

"First thing?" Rich's voice broke, disbelief surging through him. He stared at them, his vision blurring momentarily as tears stung his eyes. "If you wait until morning, they'll be long gone. Please, you have to help me now. They're just kids."

The guards exchanged uncertain glances, an awkward silence stretching painfully between them. The older man shook his head slowly, sympathy evident but restrained by duty. "I'm sorry. Protocol doesn't allow night patrols based on uncertain leads. It's too dangerous out there."

Rich stood frozen, feeling the weight of the guard's words settle like a stone in his gut. The helplessness clawed at him, sharp and cold. He swallowed hard, nodding stiffly, unable to form another word. Turning abruptly, he stepped away, the distant murmurs of apology fading quickly into silence.

He moved into the darkness, alone and numb, the realization stark and bitter: if help wouldn't come, he'd have to find them himself.

Rich hurried back toward the farm, every step heavier with grim purpose. At the house, he paused briefly, staring into the shadowed doorway, feeling the emptiness waiting inside. The familiar space now felt foreign, marked by a cold silence that only deepened the ache in his chest. He shook off the feeling, refusing to linger, his determination pushing him forward.

Inside, Rich moved swiftly and methodically. He grabbed a sturdy bag, quickly filling it with essentials—spare clothing, a water flask, dried food, and the sharp, reliable hunting knife his father had once used. His movements were precise, driven by urgency yet careful not to waste a second.

As he packed, memories of Mita's laughter and Hagan's playful teasing pressed painfully against his consciousness. He tightened his jaw, forcing the images aside, knowing any hesitation could cost him precious time.

Slinging the bag over his shoulder, Rich stepped back outside, eyes scanning the faint trail he had discovered earlier. He crouched by the disturbed earth, fingertips brushing over the footprints, their direction clear. They led away from the farm, toward the dense woods—territory he had always been wary of. Territory rumored to shelter the kind of people who stole children in the night.

Rich took a slow, steadying breath, rising to his feet. The morning chill was sharp, biting through his coat, yet his resolve hardened further. He stepped forward cautiously, entering the thick, shadowed forest with senses heightened and nerves taut.

Every sound seemed amplified—the rustling leaves beneath his feet, the distant calls of unseen animals, the quiet whisper of wind through the trees.

As he moved deeper, Rich noticed subtle signs of human passage: broken branches, disturbed foliage, and the occasional faint boot print partially obscured by leaves. Each discovery tightened the knot of tension within him, sharpening his awareness. The woods grew denser around him, the path narrowing until it was nearly indistinguishable, forcing him to rely on instinct and fleeting glimpses of the faint trail.

After several hours of slow, deliberate progress, Rich paused briefly, his body aching from the sustained tension. He leaned against a tree, scanning the area carefully, noting a crude symbol carved roughly into the bark. His fingers traced the mark—a jagged line intersected by a circle—and unease stirred within him, but he couldn't quite pinpoint why.

Drawing a quiet breath, Rich pushed onward, each step heavier than the last, driven by desperation to reclaim what was stolen from him. The faint trail led onward, deeper into territory he knew was hostile, dangerous, and utterly unfamiliar. Yet he pressed on, determined to face whatever awaited ahead.

As darkness deepened in the forest, Rich's exhaustion became overwhelming, forcing him to halt for the night. He chose a concealed spot, shielded by dense brush and low-hanging branches, carefully ensuring minimal visibility from any potential observers. With swift, quiet movements, he prepared a small, unobtrusive campsite—just enough to allow him to rest without sacrificing alertness.

Rich settled cautiously against a sturdy tree trunk, knife close at hand. The night air grew colder, seeping through his clothing and settling into his bones. Every shadow seemed alive, every distant noise amplified by his heightened senses. He closed his eyes briefly, desperately seeking rest yet unable to shake the persistent tension that gripped him. Sleep came slowly, uneasy and fitful, haunted by whispered memories and indistinct fears.

Rich startled awake at first light, heart racing as the forest slowly took shape around him in the dim dawn glow. He remained motionless, listening carefully, senses straining for any sign of danger. Gradually, the tense silence convinced him he was alone, and he cautiously sat up, muscles stiff and sore from the restless night.

Gathering his belongings swiftly and quietly, Rich rose to his feet, stretching briefly before resuming his careful, deliberate pace through the dense woods. The trail he had followed grew clearer as daylight strengthened, scattered signs of recent human passage now unmistakable—discarded wrappers, fresh boot prints, and snapped twigs.

After nearly two hours of cautious travel, Rich paused sharply, hearing muffled voices nearby. Instantly alert, he pressed himself silently against the rough bark of a wide tree, peering carefully toward the source of the sound. Through gaps in the foliage, he glimpsed figures gathered around a modest campsite. Their clothing was rough, mismatched, clearly marking them as raiders.

Before he could retreat, rough hands seized him from behind, wrenching him violently from his hiding spot. Rich struggled instinctively, but the grip only tightened, multiple strong hands pulling him roughly into the open.

"Who do we have here?" asked a low, gravelly voice from the campfire. A tall, weathered man rose slowly, regarding Rich with a cold, evaluating stare.

Rich steadied himself quickly, forcing his breathing to remain even, mind racing to formulate a believable response. "I got separated from my group," he began cautiously, voice steady despite the tension gripping his body. "We were scouting, looking for supplies. Got caught by a patrol. I managed to slip away, but I lost track of the others."

The leader's eyes narrowed skeptically, stepping closer. "Someone your size?" The man's gaze flitted around Rich's towering form as if measuring him for something. "I find that hard to believe. Your group—another raider crew? And exactly which crew might that be?"

Rich hesitated deliberately, feigning reluctance. "Small group. We move around a lot. Try staying clear of the strongholds." He allowed a hint of bitterness and resignation to enter his voice, carefully masking any sign of Coalition affiliation.

The raider studied him closely, exchanging glances with the others before finally nodding slightly. "Tie him up and keep watch. We'll see if his story checks out," he ordered sharply.

Rich's wrists were quickly bound, and he was pushed roughly to the ground near the campfire. He sat silently, eyes scanning the camp discreetly, mind sharp with determination, knowing he would need every bit of cunning and caution to survive and find his siblings.

Chapter 5 – Blood and Bindings

Rich's wrists burned from the rough bindings as he tested them subtly, muscles flexing beneath his sleeves. The raider camp stirred into action around him, morning routines breaking the deceptive calm of the night. Voices called sharply, orders barked, accompanied by the metallic clink of weapons and gear.

He was kept sitting against a gnarled tree stump, guarded loosely but continuously. His captors—weathered men and women in mismatched clothing and scavenged armor—moved with practiced ease. Their eyes rarely met his, except to offer cold indifference or mild curiosity.

Rich remained quiet, observing closely. These were the first raiders he'd ever seen up close, and he struggled to interpret their actions. His mind, shaped by the practical knowledge of farming and survival, noted simple, mundane details: cooking fires sputtered, pots of water boiled, knives sharpened methodically against rough stones. They weren't soldiers, but they were practiced and disciplined in their own harsh way.

Near the campfire, their leader stood conferring with several others. He was a tall, broad-shouldered man with a heavy brow and harsh eyes. His movements and tone conveyed authority through fear more than respect. The others around him maintained a careful distance, their eyes flicking frequently toward him, waiting for his mood to shift.

Rich felt his jaw clench involuntarily. Though he didn't know the man's name, cruelty radiated from him, evident in the careful deliberateness of his every action. He spoke quietly to those around him, yet their reactions were immediate—fearful obedience masking their faces.

He shifted uncomfortably, the bindings digging further into his wrists. A shadow fell across him, and Rich glanced upward. A younger raider, lean with sharp features and short-cropped hair, crouched nearby. His eyes—alert but slightly curious—studied Rich carefully.

"You're bigger than most we see out here," the young raider said quietly, his tone cautious but not openly hostile.

Rich met his gaze steadily. "And?"

The raider's mouth twitched into an uncertain half-smile. "Just an observation. Size can be a blessing or a curse here."

Rich narrowed his eyes slightly, keeping his voice measured. "Guess we'll find out."

"Just keep quiet. They haven't decided what to do with you yet, and that's never good."

Rich stayed silent, watching the man rise and return to the group around the leader, their conversation becoming more animated. He knew instinctively that his time here would be short and possibly brutal unless something changed drastically.

He settled back slightly against the rough bark, careful eyes taking in the camp, marking possible escape routes and vulnerabilities. His farmer's mind saw practical things—a discarded blade, ropes frayed from constant use, a loose wooden stake driven into the soft ground nearby. Simple details might mean survival.

Hours passed slowly, the sun creeping higher and intensifying the heat, sweat gathering at the small of Rich's back. He watched the raiders closely, their routines methodical but not military precise. Small arguments broke out occasionally, sharp words and tense postures quickly suppressed by a sharp glance from their leader.

Rich noticed one of the raiders, an older woman with a wiry build, moving with an obvious limp. She carried water from a small creek at the camp's edge, stumbling slightly each time she returned with the heavy bucket. Another raider—a thin, nervous-looking man—constantly fidgeted with the straps on his scavenged armor, the worn leather clearly irritating him.

Midday came, and Rich felt the burning ache in his bound wrists intensify. He shifted slightly, trying to find relief, but a sharp glare from the raider watching him stilled him again. Hunger gnawed at his stomach, but he pushed it aside, focusing instead on the patterns of his captors, marking their numbers and habits.

The leader approached him abruptly, his heavy steps crunching through the dried leaves. His dark eyes, filled with calculation and coldness, studied Rich carefully.

"You're no soldier," he said flatly, crouching to Rich's eye level. "You don't carry yourself like one."

Rich kept silent, holding the man's gaze steadily, his jaw set firmly.

"Maybe a farmer," the leader continued, amusement flickering in his eyes. "Someone who thought he could slip through unnoticed."

Rich didn't answer immediately, sensing the trap in any reply he might give. After a tense moment, he spoke carefully. "I'm no threat to you. Let me go, and you'll never see me again."

The leader chuckled, a low, humorless sound. "That's not how we do things here."

"I have nothing you want," Rich countered evenly. "Keeping me around just wastes your resources."

The leader's amusement faded, replaced by something darker. He leaned in closer, voice lowering dangerously. "You misunderstand. You are a resource. Every person we encounter has some value—even if it's just to serve as a lesson to others."

Rich met his stare directly, unwilling to show fear despite his pounding heart. "I'm more trouble than I'm worth."

The leader's eyes narrowed further, considering. "Maybe," he conceded slowly, a cruel smile spreading across his lips. "But we can't just let people wander away, spreading word about where we are."

Rich felt a surge of desperation mix with defiance. "I won't say anything. I have nothing to gain from betraying you."

The leader rose slowly, straightening to his full imposing height. "Trust," he said coldly, "is a luxury we can't afford."

He turned sharply to his group, voice rising slightly. "Get rid of him. Quietly. We move at dusk."

Rich's heart pounded sharply, his muscles tightening instinctively against the bindings. He drew a slow breath, eyes darting quickly to the frayed ropes and discarded blade once more. A quiet resolve settled over him, chasing away fear.

Two raiders approached him, their expressions indifferent, one gripping a knife loosely at his side, the other holding a battered rifle at the ready. Rich tensed, knowing any sudden movement would end his life instantly, which seemed to be nothing more than a question of timing at this point.

"Stand up," the raider with the knife ordered gruffly, nudging him roughly with a boot.

Rich rose slowly, deliberately, muscles taut with suppressed tension. He felt the second raider move behind him, tightening the bindings sharply. Pain flared through his wrists, making him wince but he refused to give them further satisfaction.

"Walk," the first raider said, gesturing toward the edge of the camp.

Rich moved forward, his steps deliberate but reluctant, eyes scanning desperately for any advantage, any possible way to escape. Every step seemed heavier than the last, carrying him closer to an inevitable and grim conclusion. His mind flitted to Hagan and

Mita, and his heart sunk with the dour reality that likely they, and now he, faced.

Just as they reached the tree line, sharp cracks suddenly rang out from the surrounding woods—gunshots shattering the tense silence. Chaos erupted instantly. The raiders around him shouted in alarm, scattering for cover, their attention torn away from their grim assignment.

He dropped instinctively, pressing himself flat against the ground as gunfire echoed around him. Through the confusion, he saw shadowy figures emerging swiftly from the trees, firing methodically and precisely into the raiders' ranks.

Rich remained still, heart hammering, mind racing. Another raider group had attacked, swift and brutal, their assault well-coordinated.

Amidst the turmoil, he felt a brief, uncertain hope surge within him. This could be his only chance for survival.

Gunfire echoed relentlessly, the acrid smell of smoke and powder thickening the air. Shouts of confusion and anger erupted from the raiders around him as they scrambled for cover, firing wildly at their assailants hidden among the trees.

Seizing the momentary distraction, Rich rolled onto his side, scanning desperately for a weapon, anything he could use. Nearby, a fallen raider lay motionless, his rifle just inches from his limp fingers. Rich crawled quickly, first securing a knife from the man's belt and quickly cutting his bindings. Then, he grabbed the weapon awkwardly, feeling its unfamiliar weight in his trembling hands.

He pushed himself upright, heart pounding furiously. He aimed clumsily at the nearest raider—the man who had been about to end his life moments earlier—and squeezed the trigger. The recoil jolted him backward, but the shot struck true, sending the raider sprawling into the dirt.

Adrenaline surged through Rich, driving out fear and hesitation. He fired again, this time at another raider sprinting for cover, barely noticing the sting in his wrists from the broken bindings. Hope surged stronger within him, the thought racing through his mind—his stronghold had found him. They had come to save him.

He aimed again.

Click

The rifle clicked uselessly, the magazine empty. Panic flashed through Rich, quickly replaced by determination. He tossed the weapon aside, his massive frame tensed for close combat.

A raider lunged at him, brandishing a knife. Rich pivoted sharply, using his superior bulk and strength to grapple the man's wrist, forcing the blade away. With a swift motion, he slammed his shoulder into the attacker, sending him sprawling to the ground.

Breathing heavily, Rich turned again, senses alert. The battle around him was fierce, bodies clashing, fists flying, knives flashing. Another raider came at him from behind, trying to catch him off guard. Rich spun swiftly, catching the raider by the throat and hoisting him off his feet, before hurling him forcefully to the ground.

He stood, muscles heaving with exertion, eyes wild with adrenaline and survival instinct. Around him, the attacking force steadily pushed the remaining raiders back, the chaos beginning to settle into a grim victory. Despite the exhaustion creeping into his limbs, Rich stood firm, ready to face whatever came next.

Another raider charged toward Rich, yelling in fury. Rich met him head-on, the two colliding heavily. Rich absorbed the impact, driving his attacker backward, his size and raw strength giving him the advantage. He threw a powerful punch, connecting solidly and knocking the raider senseless to the dirt.

Rich stood, breathing heavily, eyes darting quickly around the chaotic aftermath. His heart hammered in his chest, and for a moment he scanned the faces of the new arrivals, desperately searching for someone—anyone—he might recognize. His initial hope quickly turned to confusion, then dread.

These weren't coalition soldiers. They wore mismatched armor, their faces hardened by survival, eyes cold and calculating. They were raiders. Just another group of raiders.

A sinking realization took hold of him just as a calm, almost pleasant if not for its cold tone, voice broke through the tension. "Impressive. Very impressive."

Rich turned slowly, his eyes landing on a tall, lean man standing calmly several feet away, a Vanguard trexium rifle leveled steadily at Rich's chest. The man's expression was composed, almost amused, his voice unsettlingly smooth.

"You're quite effective, aren't you?" the man observed mildly. "What's your name, friend?"

Rich steadied himself, wariness thickening his voice. "Rich."

The man's eyebrows lifted slightly. "Rich. I'm Evo." He gestured vaguely with the rifle toward the fallen raiders. "Sorry about all this. Kael and I had a... disagreement. Unfortunately, you've found yourself right in the middle of its resolution."

Rich remained silent, muscles tense, watching Evo carefully.

"Relax," Evo said gently, though the rifle never wavered. "The fight is over. Kael and his men are dealt with. I'm curious, though—how did someone like you end up here, with them? You look like you belong behind the walls, not out here in the forests."

Rich hesitated, weighing his words cautiously. "Didn't have much choice."

Evo smiled faintly, nodding understandingly. "That's usually how it goes out here. Well, Rich, you've earned my attention today. I'm curious to see what you're capable of."

Rich swallowed, eyes never leaving Evo's face. "And if I'm not interested?"

"If I didn't think we could use you, you'd already be dead." Evo said casually, almost with a joke in his tone.

Rich clenched his jaw, meeting Evo's gaze steadily despite the tight knot forming in his chest. "If that's your plan, get it over with. I've already seen enough death today."

Evo regarded Rich thoughtfully for a long moment, the rifle lowering slightly. "Death is easy. Finding someone useful out here—that's harder." He tilted his head slightly, a curious smile forming. "Come with us. You're strong, capable, and clearly willing to do what it takes to survive. You might find our way of life suits you better than you think."

Rich hesitated, his thoughts briefly flickering back to his siblings. Every instinct urged caution, but reality gave him little choice. Survival meant making difficult decisions.

"Fine," Rich said quietly, his voice firm but wary. "I'll go with you—for now."

Evo's smile widened, genuine approval briefly lighting his eyes. "Good choice, Rich. Welcome to the group."

Chapter 6 – Stolen and Sold

Rich followed Evo and his raiders into their camp, a makeshift settlement hidden deep within the dense cover of the forest. The camp was rough and utilitarian, structures patched together from scavenged materials—sheet metal, worn canvas, and timber. Despite raiders' well-known distaste for the Strongholds, Rich noted with irony that they'd fashioned something remarkably similar here. Makeshift barriers, lookout posts, and fire lines had been arranged with clear purpose. Security, it seemed, had its value even among those who openly scorned Coalition life. After all, the undead didn't discriminate between raiders and coalition forces.

Eyes tracked Rich carefully as he moved through the camp, suspicion and curiosity mixing openly in their stares. Evo spoke briefly to a raider near the center of the encampment—a stocky man with a permanently furrowed brow and narrowed, cautious eyes Rich learned was named Hale. Hale wore his armor meticulously, the scraps carefully reinforced with leather stitching, and his movements were always deliberate, every step precise.

"He stays with us, but keep him disarmed and closely watched," Evo instructed firmly, his voice quiet but authoritative. "Until we know more about him."

Rich didn't protest, knowing it would be useless and might only make his situation worse. Instead, he silently took in his surroundings, trying to gauge the dynamics at play within Evo's group. Raiders moved about their tasks—sharpening weapons, repairing gear, or cooking meals over smoky fires—with a wary efficiency born from constant survival.

"Over here," Hale ordered Rich gruffly, motioning him toward a small, empty tent at the edge of the camp. Hale's voice carried an edge of authority and cautious distrust, though there was something methodical and almost respectful in how he treated even prisoners. "This'll be your place. Don't wander off. You won't get far, anyway."

Rich nodded silently, stepping into the sparse shelter and sitting down heavily. Alone, he allowed himself a slow, deep breath, the weight of recent events pressing heavily on his shoulders. His wrists ached, raw from the earlier bindings, and fatigue seeped deep into his bones.

As dusk settled over the camp, Rich watched through the flap of the tent, eyes cautious but observant. Raiders gathered around central fires, their conversations low and tense. Among them was a wiry, sharp-featured woman with close-cropped hair named Kara, whose laughter, though rare, always carried genuine warmth despite her hard exterior. Beside her, a lanky, jittery young man named Sid, with nervous eyes and quick hands, stoked the fire constantly, never fully at ease.

Rich recognized clearly that he was an outsider, and trust would not come quickly. Through the shadows, Rich noticed Evo moving calmly through the camp, exchanging quiet words with various raiders. The respect Evo commanded was clear, though whether it came from genuine loyalty or fear, Rich couldn't yet tell.

Rich settled back on the rough bedding provided, mind racing through his limited options. Survival meant cooperation—at least for now. He would have to watch, learn, and wait patiently for any chance to regain control of his fate.

Days began to blur together as Rich found himself settling into a cautious routine within Evo's camp. He awoke each morning early, immediately put to work on mundane tasks: hauling water from the nearby creek, repairing worn gear, or chopping firewood under Hale's watchful eyes. The raiders kept him under constant, cautious observation, clearly unwilling to trust him fully, yet slowly accepting his presence as necessary.

During these daily chores, Rich carefully observed the group, noting the subtle dynamics at play. Kara often lingered nearby, never speaking much, but offering him brief nods of acknowledgment. Her sharp eyes seemed to miss nothing, and though she maintained a tough exterior, Rich occasionally caught glimpses of genuine compassion in her interactions with younger, less experienced raiders. It almost reminded him of how his mother had looked at Mita.

Sid remained wary, often jittery and suspicious. Yet Rich noticed Sid's hands moved with impressive skill whenever repairs were needed, his nervousness fading whenever his mind was occupied by detailed work. Rich came to recognize Sid's anxiety as a coping mechanism—always vigilant, always cautious, never fully at rest.

Among the raiders, Rich noticed one who stood apart from the rest. He had heard the man's name from others talking to him. Leron, lean and quiet, kept mostly to himself, observing rather than participating in idle conversation. Rich often caught Leron watching him from a distance, though always discreetly, as if measuring him carefully from afar. Unlike the others, he seemed neither openly hostile nor wary—just cautiously interested.

One afternoon, as Rich carefully patched a torn canvas tent under Hale's supervision, Leron finally approached quietly. Having maintained his distance until now, Leron offered a cautious smile as he knelt to assist with the repairs.

"You're picking things up quickly," Leron remarked lightly, his voice conversational but careful. "Better than most new arrivals."

Rich glanced up, cautiously meeting Leron's gaze. "I didn't realize I had a choice."

Leron chuckled softly, nodding. "Fair point." His hands moved deftly, stitching fabric with practiced ease. "Look, everyone here has a story—a reason they're not in a stronghold. But if you keep your head down and do your work, eventually you'll become one of us."

Rich considered his words carefully, his voice low. "And if that's not what I want?"

Leron's hands paused momentarily before resuming their careful work. "Then you fake it, outsider. Survival is about adaptation. Give the people here enough reason to trust you, and you'll earn some freedom. After that…well, decisions become easier."

Rich fell silent, absorbing Leron's advice. He recognized its practicality, even if he resented the necessity. As days passed, he would have to decide what freedom truly meant, and how far he was willing to go to regain it.

As time passed, Rich gradually found himself earning a measure of cautious trust within Evo's group. The tasks assigned to him became more varied, moving from purely manual labor to responsibilities that required careful attention and discretion. He still wasn't allowed weapons, but fewer eyes tracked his every move, signaling a shift in their perception of him from immediate threat to tentative ally.

Each night, as Rich sat near the firelight with the others, he found his mind inevitably drifting to his siblings. The image of Mita's brave, defiant stare and Hagan's bright, trusting eyes haunted him, fueling a constant, simmering restlessness. He knew integration into Evo's group was necessary for his survival, but his true goal remained clear and unchanging—to find his siblings and leave this place behind.

One quiet evening, as embers crackled gently and shadows danced on the faces around him, Rich found himself sitting beside Leron. Trust had slowly begun to form between them, built through brief, careful conversations and shared tasks.

"Leron," Rich began quietly, voice low and cautious, "what does it take to leave here? If someone wanted to move on, what would Evo say?"

Leron glanced sideways at Rich, thoughtful and guarded. "Depends," he replied after a moment. "If Evo trusts you completely, maybe he'd let you go. But that takes a long time. And he doesn't trust easily."

Rich hesitated, choosing his next words carefully. "I can't stay here forever. I have... people out there, people I need to find."

Leron nodded slowly, his expression sympathetic but wary. "Be careful, Rich. Evo doesn't like losing things he values. Right now, you're useful. But if he thinks you'll run off..."

"I understand," Rich murmured, leaning back slightly, eyes focused on the shifting firelight. Internally, he resolved to remain patient, to build enough trust to earn his freedom, no matter how long or difficult that path might become. Each day was a careful balance—earning the raiders' trust without losing sight of the only goal that truly mattered.

The firelight flickered softly, casting elongated shadows that danced across the encampment's rough shelters and makeshift tents. Rich sat quietly beside Leron, their usual guarded silence momentarily easing into something more reflective. The warmth from the fire did little to dispel the chill that settled in Rich's chest, brought on by his persistent worry for his siblings.

Leron prodded the embers with a stick, his face thoughtful, the orange glow highlighting deep lines that seemed out of place on someone so young. Finally, he spoke, voice barely audible above the gentle crackling of the flames.

"You remind me of myself when I first joined up," Leron began softly, eyes fixed on the smoldering wood. "Restless. Always looking for something outside these walls."

Rich glanced at Leron curiously, sensing there was more beneath the casual admission. "Did you find it?" he asked quietly.

Leron's eyes darkened slightly, his expression turning distant. "No," he admitted after a heavy pause. "I had a sister. Lilah. She was ten. Sweet kid, always laughing, always hopeful, even when things got bad. I did everything I could to protect her, but—" He stopped abruptly, jaw clenching tightly as he swallowed hard.

Rich remained silent, waiting patiently for Leron to continue. The pain on his companion's face was raw, unmistakable. Finally, Leron exhaled slowly, regaining his composure.

"There was a raid. I was out gathering supplies, left her in a hiding spot we'd used a hundred times before. Thought she'd be safe." Leron's voice trembled slightly. "When I got back, she was gone. Raiders took her, or maybe worse. I never found out. I searched for months until Evo's group found me, half-starved, nearly dead. Evo gave me purpose, a reason to survive."

Rich felt a heavy weight settle in his chest, deeply moved by the pain in Leron's voice. "I'm sorry," he murmured sincerely.

Leron met Rich's eyes, a faint, understanding nod bridging the gap between their stories. "Don't give up hope. Whoever it is you're looking for," Leron said softly. "But be careful. Hope can be dangerous if it blinds you to what's real."

Rich nodded slowly, the advice sinking in alongside the unspoken bond forming between them. Together they sat quietly, lost in thought, each man drawing strength from the other's quiet, shared understanding.

Days passed quietly, each one blending seamlessly into the next as Rich continued to perform his tasks around Evo's camp. Gradually, the rhythm of raider life began to feel strangely familiar—routine chores interspersed with brief moments of camaraderie and cautious trust. Rich observed the dynamics carefully, noting how alliances formed and shifted, how power subtly asserted itself through small gestures and shared looks.

He watched the raiders prepare their gear meticulously, reinforcing armor and sharpening blades with practiced skill. Meals were communal, simple fare cooked over open fires, everyone gathering to eat together, though the conversations remained mostly superficial—survival tips, past encounters, occasional laughter. It was a harsh but functioning community built on mutual necessity more than genuine friendship.

One night, Rich found himself sitting around the larger fire at the center of the camp. Raiders sat scattered around, their faces illuminated by the flickering flames, their voices relaxed in the rare moment of rest.

Rich was quietly contemplating his next move when snippets of a nearby conversation suddenly drew his attention.

"Whatever happened with those two kids, anyway?" a raider named Sid asked casually, nudging another raider beside him.

"The ones we got from that farm?" Kara replied, shaking her head slightly. "Evo sold them off to another group."

Rich froze, the blood in his veins turning to ice as his heart thudded painfully in his chest.

Another raider shrugged dismissively. "They were too much trouble. Most kids are. Better to sell 'em off, let someone else deal with their whining."

"Feisty kids, though," Kara added with a chuckle, her voice oddly amused. "Unless they changed their attitudes, whoever bought them probably tossed them to the walkers by now."

Laughter rippled briefly through the group, the sound sharp and cruel in Rich's ears. He fought to maintain a neutral expression, his fists clenching tightly at his sides, every muscle tense with barely controlled rage.

Rich stared into the fire, jaw locked tight, forcing himself to breathe evenly. The quiet conversation around him faded into a muffled hum as he grappled silently with the horror of what he'd just learned, his mind consumed by grief and burning determination.

Chapter 7 – A Bitter Harvest

Rich's breathing came in short, ragged bursts as he stepped away from the fire, fists clenched tightly at his sides. He moved quickly, retreating to the quiet shadow of his tent, away from prying eyes and casual cruelty. Inside, he dropped heavily onto the rough bedding, his head spinning with shock and fury.

The raiders' laughter echoed harshly in his ears, replaying endlessly, blending cruelly with the images of Mita's determined face and Hagan's wide, trusting eyes. They'd been taken—sold off like animals, traded away because they were "too much trouble." Rich felt his chest tighten, grief choking him as the reality of their fate settled in with grim finality.

His eyes stung, burning with tears that he refused to let fall. Anger built inside him, a white-hot rage that slowly overshadowed the pain. His hands shook, muscles tensed as an unfamiliar coldness settled into his bones—a sharp clarity that cut through the confusion and grief.

Rich rose slowly, determination hardening his features. He had played their game, had earned their trust just enough to stay alive. But now he understood clearly: the raiders had never truly been allies, never truly safe. They were monsters who had robbed him of his family.

He drew a slow, steadying breath, calming the storm within just enough to think clearly. Rich knew what needed to be done. Tonight, the façade would end. Tonight, Rich would become something more than a farmer forced to survive among raiders.

Tonight, Rich would bring justice for his siblings.

Night deepened around the camp, cloaking it in darkness punctuated only by faint firelight and murmured conversations. Rich moved quietly, stepping carefully from his tent, blending into shadows cast by tents and makeshift shelters. His heartbeat quickened, each step deliberate, each breath controlled.

His eyes focused sharply on Evo's tent near the camp's center, knowing exactly what he sought there—the Vanguard rifle, a prize Evo always kept close. Rich had seen it countless times, hanging from a simple rack beside Evo's cot, a symbol of power and authority. Tonight, it would serve a different purpose.

Slipping silently past tents and sleeping raiders, Rich felt a strange calm descend over him. The camp was familiar now; he knew its patterns, its weaknesses. He paused, holding his breath as a sentry passed obliviously nearby, before continuing his steady advance.

Reaching Evo's tent, Rich hesitated only briefly, listening carefully for signs of movement within. Hearing nothing but deep, steady breathing, he slowly parted the canvas flap and stepped inside. Evo lay asleep, unaware and vulnerable, with the prized trexium rifle hanging within easy reach.

Rich's fingers closed around the rifle's grip, feeling its reassuring weight and cold precision. A surge of strength coursed through him, fueled by vengeance and resolve. Carefully lifting the weapon, he backed quietly from the tent, heart pounding but resolve unwavering.

Outside, under the clear night sky, Rich paused briefly, gripping the rifle firmly. He felt no hesitation now, only a grim certainty that this night would redefine his place in this harsh world.

Taking a deep breath, he stepped purposefully forward into the darkness, ready to confront the monsters who had stolen what was left of his family.

Rich moved cautiously, each step guided by determination and quiet desperation. The rifle felt heavy and unfamiliar in his grip, its awkwardness reminding him sharply that he was a farmer—not a soldier. His thoughts were clear but filled with anxiety, driven by the memories of his siblings and the bitter betrayal he'd uncovered.

He approached the first sentry carefully, using the shadows and terrain to his advantage. Rather than precision, it was patience and quiet, steady caution that served him best. The raider, relaxed and unaware, sat staring lazily into the darkness, oblivious to the threat behind him. Rich, heart pounding, raised the heavy rifle and struck swiftly, using sheer force born of years laboring in fields and hauling heavy equipment. The man collapsed, stunned and silent, as Rich quickly moved on.

He paused often, hiding behind tents and stacks of supplies, watching for patterns and opportunities, each step a cautious calculation. As a farmer, Rich understood rhythm and routine, patiently observing until he saw openings in their makeshift defenses.

The next raider, distracted by tending to a fire, didn't see Rich approach from behind, a quick swing with the rifle knocking him unconscious without a struggle. Rich moved deliberately, using his knowledge of the camp layout to approach raiders one by one, never giving them a chance to sound the alarm.

It was only when a raider stumbled unexpectedly from a tent, their eyes meeting Rich's in stunned recognition, that the quiet unraveled. Rich, adrenaline surging, raised the rifle clumsily, his shot echoing loudly through the camp, shattering the fragile silence.

Panic erupted as raiders woke, confused shouts filling the air. Rich abandoned stealth, forced now to rely on raw strength and determination rather than precision. Raiders came at him, disorganized but aggressive, and he met each challenge with sheer brute force, his large frame giving him the crucial advantage.

Suddenly, Evo emerged from the chaos, stepping forward with hands raised slightly, a calming smile on his face. "Rich," Evo called smoothly, his voice steady despite the turmoil around him. "Listen to me. I know you're angry, I don't know what about, but let's talk. This doesn't have to end badly. Think about it—there's still a place for you here. We can make this right."

Rich stared at Evo coldly, the honeyed words grating painfully against his raw nerves. His mind flashed with memories of Evo's calculated cruelty, the indifferent smirks, the casual disregard for life that had destroyed Rich's family. Evo opened his mouth to speak again, confidence unwavering. "Rich, listen—this is a misunderstanding, we can still—"

The words ended abruptly as Rich fired without hesitation.

Evo's expression barely had time to register shock before he fell, silenced mid-sentence. Rich lowered the weapon slowly, feeling no remorse—only a profound, weary certainty. It was Evo's decisions that had brought them all to this point, and Rich was simply finishing what they had started.

Rich stood over Evo's fallen body, his breathing ragged, the echo of the rifle shot still ringing sharply in his ears. Chaos continued to swirl around him as surviving raiders scrambled to respond, confusion and panic evident in their frantic movements. Determination steeled Rich once again, his large frame propelling him forward with purpose and raw strength.

He pressed deeper into the camp, neutralizing threats as they appeared. Each confrontation was brief, decisive, driven by desperation rather than skill. Rich's farmer's ingenuity showed clearly—he used terrain to his advantage, improvised cover from crates and overturned carts, and struck swiftly, capitalizing on surprise and the chaos around him.

As he turned a corner, Rich froze suddenly, confronted by a familiar face. Leron stood facing him, weapon raised defensively, eyes wide with confusion and shock.

"Rich," Leron's voice was unsteady, disbelief clouding his expression. "What are you doing? Why?"

Rich's grip tightened on the rifle, heart heavy with anguish. "You took them, Leron," he managed, voice thick with grief and accusation. "My family. My siblings. Sold them like animals."

Realization slowly spread across Leron's face, sorrow mingling with pain. "I didn't know, Rich. I swear, I didn't know it was your family."

"But you knew they took someone's," Rich countered, his tone cold, unforgiving. "And you did nothing."

Leron shook his head desperately, lowering his weapon slightly, his eyes pleading. "Please, Rich. You're not like this. You're better than this."

Rich met Leron's gaze, the weight of betrayal and grief tearing at his resolve. His heart ached, knowing the friendship they'd built had been real, genuine. But the memories of Mita and Hagan overwhelmed him, drowning out any hesitation.

Leron barely opened his mouth to respond when Rich fired. The sound echoed, final and absolute, and Leron crumpled silently to the ground, disbelief still etched across his features.

Rich stood motionless for a long moment, the weight of his action settling heavily upon him. Finally, he turned away, shoulders slumped beneath the enormity of it all, knowing there was no turning back from the path he had chosen.

Rich sank heavily to his knees at the edge of the camp, exhaustion and grief overwhelming him. Flames rose high, consuming the tents and structures, their angry light flickering over the silent, scattered bodies. Smoke filled the air, thick and acrid, curling upward into the dark sky.

He stared numbly into the flames, the weight of his actions pressing on his mind and into his conscience. The noise, the violence, the chaos—all of it would soon draw the undead, walkers hungry and relentless. Rich no longer cared. He had accomplished his vengeance, but at a cost he had barely begun to comprehend.

And in the end, he remained alone, with no clearer path to finding his siblings, who were more than likely dead, than before his run in with Kael and then Evo.

The distant rustle of branches and leaves stirred him from his grim contemplation. Rich closed his eyes, resigned to the fate approaching steadily from the shadows. But instead of the shambling, dragging steps of walkers, a different sound pierced the night—the unmistakable hum of flyer engines, growing steadily louder.

Rich opened his eyes, lifting his head slowly in confusion and disbelief. Bright beams of light cut sharply through the darkness, and moments later, figures descended swiftly from above, their jetpacks illuminating the clearing in sharp bursts of pink and white.

One soldier landed close, rifle raised cautiously as he scanned the dark clearing. Spotting Rich's silhouette in the dim firelight, he called out cautiously, "Survivor here!"

Another soldier landed swiftly, joining him and illuminating Rich's face with a handheld light. Recognition dawned quickly in the second soldier's eyes. "Wait—this is the missing farmer. We found him."

The first soldier immediately lowered his weapon and approached Rich carefully, extending a steady hand. "Up you get. We've got you."

Rich remained silent as the soldiers gently lifted him, taking the vanguard rifle still gripped in his hands. Tears blurred his vision, falling silently down his face as the weight of his losses—family, friends, and even the inevitability of death he'd anticipated—pressed heavily upon him.

As they guided him toward an opening where larger airships could come pull them out, Rich cast one final glance over his shoulder at the burning camp. Flames crackled and danced, illuminating the wreckage of a life he had briefly known, and had himself destroyed. Leron's face and expression of betrayal haunted the space between blinks of his eyes. A sobering realization settled in his chest—this was the end of one journey and the uncertain beginning of another. Deep within, he acknowledged bitterly that he had lost sight of who he once was, replaced now by someone forged in fire and grief, uncertain if he could ever reclaim the simpler life of the farmer he used to be.

Chapter 8 – Burials Without Graves

The airship's engines ran in a low, even thrum, steady enough that Rich could feel the vibration in his teeth. The bench webbing cut into his shoulder where it crossed his chest, the fabric stiff and faintly tacky with oil. He kept his eyes on the floor between his boots, the scuffed metal patterned with old scratches and darker stains that had worked too deep to ever clean.

Someone passed down the aisle—weight shifting with the slight sway of the deck—and checked the straps without looking at his face. A ration pack landed on the bench beside him a few minutes later, the seal crinkling in the quiet. Rich left it there. The smell of scorched canvas and burned flesh still sat at the back of his throat, and there was no space in him for food.

When he finally glanced toward the viewport, the stronghold was already taking shape against the dark. First the towers—square, heavy things with trexium light bleeding at the seams. Then the walls, panels mismatched and scarred from moves and hits alike, each weld line catching the airship's running lights in brief silver flashes.

The landing struts hit the pad with a hollow metallic groan, followed by the sharp hiss of hydraulics bleeding pressure. The ramp dropped, letting in air colder than it should have been, tinged with dust and the faint static scent of the perimeter shield. The soldiers ahead moved quick, boots ringing against the ramp before their steps were swallowed by the yard.

A medic took his arm, guiding him without hurry but without pause. The med bay was just off the yard, its door propped to let traffic move through. Inside, the lights were sharp enough to pull a flinch out of him, cutting clean through the smell of boiled linen and antiseptic. They had him on a cot in seconds, hands moving with the practiced rhythm of people who'd seen too many like him in a single night.

Cold swabs worked grit from shallow cuts. Fingers pressed along ribs and forearms. Someone looked over an old scar at his collarbone and said nothing. Charts were marked. Gloves snapped off. A man in a quartermaster's tabard appeared in the doorway, keycard in hand.

"C-block, room twelve." He set the card in Rich's palm and was gone.

The corridor beyond the med bay felt too quiet, the sound of the yard already sealed away behind thick doors. The walls here were plain steel, paint dulled to an uneven gray, the air faintly stale under the constant hum of the recycler. His boots carried a hollow echo on the concrete until he stopped outside twelve.

The lock clicked at the keycard's touch. The room inside was square and spare—cot against one wall with its blanket folded tight, desk in the corner, chair tucked under like it had been measured. No windows. No voices. Just the same recycled air, the same low hum.

He stepped in, set the card on the desk, and sat on the edge of the cot. The springs shifted once, then stilled.

The stronghold went on without him outside these walls—engines cooling, boots moving along the gantries, orders passing down in clipped voices. In here, the quiet pressed in close, the kind that left too much space for the wrong thoughts to move in.

They came for him early, before the light in the hall had shifted to day-cycle. The door latch clicked, hinges groaned once, and a shadow filled the frame.

"Commander wants to see you," the soldier said. It wasn't a request.

Rich pulled on his coat and followed, the air in the corridor still carrying the metallic chill of the night. The hum of the recycler was steady at his back until they stepped out into the yard, where other sounds took over—boots on the gantries, the grind of a lift hauling cargo to the upper tier, voices calling to one another in short, clipped bursts.

They crossed to the admin block, where the commanders and base commander had their offices near the training grounds. The stairs were grated steel, the edges worn smooth by years of traffic, transport, and reassembly. The view from halfway up was all angles—towers squared against the dark line of the wall.

The office was high enough to see the whole yard through two wide panes, each one edged with old scratches that caught the sun. The man behind the desk didn't look up right away. He finished whatever note he was writing, set the stylus down in a careful line with the rest, and only then gave Rich his attention.

"Richard Halden," he said, as if testing how the name sat in the air.

Rich didn't answer.

The commander leaned back, studying him the way you might study a tool pulled from the bottom of a drawer—checking for cracks, for the weight in the hand. His hair was going to gray, not all at once but in lines at the temples. There was no shine to his uniform, just the wear of long use.

Behind the man stood a Vanguard, with deep red lines in his armor. Rich has seen him before, but didn't know his name. The soldiers' presence filled the room, somehow even more than his commanders.

"I read the report from the Vanguard who found you," he said finally. "You survived something most don't walk away from. Raiders. Numbers against you. You came back alive. That doesn't happen without grit, and it doesn't happen without instincts. We could use someone like you."

Rich's brow furrowed; the burn wounds and lacerations on his face stung. They'd leave their mark but the damage wouldn't leave him anything but scarred. The internal scars were worse than anything the raiders had done to his face.

Rich turned his attention away from his discomfort and towards the men in front of him. Was the man asking what Rich thought he was?

"I barely made it. I survived by fighting with pure rage over what they did to my family. It's not the same thing as being a soldier."

The commander nodded slightly, conceding the point. "No, it's not. But you didn't fold either. Most would have. That's why we're having this conversation."

Rich shifted his weight, uneasy. The words left his mouth in a flat, dry tone.

"I'm not a soldier. I've worked soil my whole life. My hands know shovels, not rifles."

"That's what training is for," the commander replied evenly. "We don't put a weapon in someone's hands and send them straight to the wall. We run a proving cycle—conditioning, weapons work, tactics. Weeks that will break you down and build you back. If you fail, you go back to your fields. If you pass, you'll have earned your place. And someone like you—I could even see in the Vanguard one day."

Rich looked down at his hands, scarred from years of labor. "And if I can't keep up?"

"You will.," said the commander flatly.

Rich's jaw tightened. "I couldn't even protect my own family. What makes you think I could protect anyone else? What makes you think I have any ability to work with anyone? Why would you want me?"

The commander leaned forward, voice low but certain. "Because you're still standing here, asking that question. Most men who lose what you lost are already gone. You're not. That tells me more than the report."

Rich stayed silent for a long moment, his forearms tense though his hands hung loose. Finally, the commander's eyes narrowed slightly. "So I'll ask you: what do you want, Halden? You could go back to your plot. Farm again. Keep your head down until it's time to pack up and move on. Or you can take this chance and see if you've got more in you than planting rows."

Rich kept his gaze on the edge of the desk. The polished metal there had been worn dull by years of hands gripping it. His father had once leaned over a similar surface in a stronghold office, maybe even this one, arguing for a better plot. Rich could almost hear it, his father's voice low but firm, hands flat as if bracing against the weight of the man across from him. That memory pressed into Rich's chest now, heavy and unwelcome. He forced it aside, drawing in a slow breath through his nose until the ache thinned.

"I'll try," he said finally.

The commander gave a single nod. "Get your affairs in order today. You'll be expected at the training yards at first light tomorrow morning."

Rich left the office to find the first pale lines of dawn edging the rooftops. The yard was waking—supply crews hauling crates from the night drops, guards trading shifts, the hiss of steam from the mess as breakfast lines formed. He crossed the yard without hurry, each step carrying him closer to the south gate and the dirt path beyond.

The path down to the farm was the same one he'd walked a hundred mornings before, though now it felt different beneath his boots. Dew clung to the grass along the ditch, wetting the edges of his trousers with each step. The sun was still climbing, thin and pale behind the ridge, and the valley air carried that damp, earthy smell that came before the heat. He should have felt comfort in it, but there was nothing left of comfort in this place.

The gate hung as it always had, chain looped once around the post. The wood was soft in places where Hagan had driven nails too close to the edge, still marked by his small, uneven hammer blows. Rich rested a hand against it for a moment, feeling the texture of the worn grain under his palm, before pushing it open. The hinge squealed like it hadn't been oiled in weeks.

The rows stretched out before him, though they weren't rows anymore. Weeds had pushed through the loose soil, thin stalks bowing under the weight of dew. The trexium relay hub at the far edge still blinked, faint through a film of dust, but there was no hum of irrigation lines, no thrum of water being pushed along the channels. He could see where the ground had settled unevenly, the ditches drying in strange curves where Mita used to fuss over them until they ran straight.

He crouched at the first row, scooping a handful of soil. It crumbled too easily, loose between his fingers. He rubbed it against his palm and let it drift back to the earth. Once, that gesture had meant assessment, promise, a farmer's ritual of measuring what could be coaxed from the ground. Now it was just dirt, falling away. It seemed a hollow task.

Inside the house the air was stale, touched faintly with the scent of smoke, taste old meals, and memories that were still too fresh to be painful yet. A chair sat out from the table, exactly as it had been on the last morning he'd eaten here. He could picture Mita sitting in it, her elbows on the wood, voice sharp as she told Hagan not to talk with his mouth full. He stepped into the kitchen. The tin cup Hagan had favored was still upside down on the counter, waiting. Someone had cleaned it, but the familiarity in its place made his chest ache.

The bedroom was stripped, the cots bare, but the crates at their feet hadn't been emptied. He crouched by Mita's first. Inside, wrapped in a scrap of cloth, were the beads she'd worn on her wrist when she worked. The twine was frayed at the edge, one bead cracked where she'd pinched it too hard threading irrigation lines.

In the other crate he found Hagan's carved goat, edges smoothed by small hands. He turned it over in his palm, feeling the shallow grooves of the knife marks.

He sat on the edge of the cot with both tokens in hand; the silence pressing down until it felt like the air itself had weight. These things weren't just reminders. They were pieces of his siblings that had survived. They hadn't. He closed his fist around them until the edges pressed into his skin, a pain that felt almost deserved.

For a moment he considered taking them. But he knew that any token, any memento of this place would be an anchor to a life that no longer existed. The weight of it would be heavier than any weapon or armor he would lift. He set the tokens on the bed near Hagan's pillow, and for a reason he couldn't quite explain, tucked the toys in as if putting them to sleep.

The farm was quiet, but it wasn't the kind of quiet that soothed. It was the quiet of abandonment. Tools left in the dirt, a door left ajar, echoes without the people who made them. He had lived his whole life in places like this, plots meant to be planted, harvested, and moved on. Yet this one felt permanent in a way the others hadn't, as if the soil itself had taken something from him he couldn't get back.

For a moment he imagined what it would be like to try again here. To reseat the pipes, drive off the weeds, turn the soil until it carried food again. His mind's eye filled with what could have been. He could almost see Mita kneeling in the dirt, her hands pink with cold as she forced the couplings tight. Hagan chasing goats along the fence. Their voices filled the room for a breath, and then they were gone, leaving him with nothing but dust and silence.

He rose slowly and walked back into the main room. His hand brushed against the table as he passed, fingertips tracing the worn edge. He could still hear the scrape of bowls, Hagan's laughter at some half-formed joke, Mita's muttered complaints about rations.

His breath caught, sharp and uneven, before he pushed the memory down.

At the doorway he paused, looking back. The chair was still out, the cup still on the counter, the light falling in through the shutters at the same angle it always had at this hour. It looked like a place someone could step back into, sit down, and start life again. But he knew that wasn't true. Without them here, it was only wood, stone and empty air.

Rich pulled the door shut behind him, the sound flat and final in the morning quiet.

Outside, he met a man holding a clipboard. Rich signed his name, the last motion of goodbye. He did it without hesitation, without emotion. This was his burial, his goodbye to his parents, to his siblings, and in his own way, to himself.

By the time he reached the gate, the dew had burned off. The weeds straightened in the sun, reclaiming the rows. He didn't look over his shoulder as he looped the chain back around the post and set his boots toward the interior of the stronghold.

Chapter 9 – The Mourners Redemption

The horn sounded sharp in the dark, rolling through the steel halls like a call dragged on the wind. Rich was already awake. He hadn't slept much — the cot was serviceable, the room clean enough, but it wasn't the silence that kept him restless. It was the anticipation, the churn of knowing that today would be his first time in the field wearing the armor he had trained for.

He pulled the black Vanguard armor from its stand; the plates catching faint light in the dim room. One by one he fitted them over his massive frame — greaves, chest, gauntlets — each piece locking into place with practiced motions until the full weight settled on his shoulders. The armor was heavy on its own before it was powered up, but it was the kind of weight he had chosen. When he lowered the helmet over his head, the seal hissed shut and the world narrowed to the quiet hum inside. The armor powered up from its trexium core, and its weight immediately balanced, assisting his movement, enhancing his speed and power. He was no longer a farmer in borrowed quarters. He was Vanguard now. At least as of a week ago.

He laced his boots, pulled his coat around him, and stepped into the corridor. The air was cool, tinged with the faint tang of trexium exhaust. Outside, the stronghold was stirring. Engines rumbled to life in the yards. Voices carried from the mess line, clipped and practical. The clang of steel doors echoed across the gantries as guards traded shifts.

Rich walked a slow lap along the interior ring, letting his eyes take in what had once felt foreign but now pressed against him with the weight of familiarity. He passed the hangars where airships sat in their cradles, crews moving around them in deliberate patterns. Beyond, training yards stretched wide, marked by fresh ruts in the dirt where drills had been run late into the night.

He paused at the range. Targets lined the far wall, distant silhouettes barely visible through the morning haze. Two recruits had already claimed lanes.

The first was a tall girl lying prone with her rifle braced against her shoulder, her body tight, shoulders squared with careful precision. Every shot she sent downrange struck clean, though a touch off center. She corrected between volleys, eyes hard and fixed on the target.

Beside her was another trainee in slate-grey armor, also prone, his movements calmer, almost methodical. He fired in measured rhythm, each report cracking against the wall. When the marks flared at the target, the pattern was so tight it nearly looked like one shot repeated. Even as the drill shifted to moving silhouettes, he didn't break stride. The girl pressed harder, jaw set, while his grouping stayed unbroken.

Rich leaned against the fence rail, watching in silence in memory of working the same drills for what felt like a lifetime. He had been good, but not as good as either of these two. If they wanted, he thought, they could make good vanguard. He had seen them in other training drills. The rifles barked again and again, the echo rolling back across the yard. Around them, other soldiers readied for the day, but here the world had narrowed to two figures and the space between their shots.

When the lane cleared and the drill ended, the recruits lowered their weapons. The girl glanced at the results, her jaw tight. The boy in grey holstered his rifle without a word, already turning away.

Rich's eyes lingered on him. That one will be a sniper, he thought. Sharp enough to matter one day.

He pushed off the rail and kept walking, boots scuffing softly against the concrete. The stronghold was alive around him— the hum of machinery, the rhythm of soldiers, the pulse of something larger than any one man.

By the time Rich finished his lap and returned to C-block, the yard had fully woken. The mess line stretched out the door, soldiers shouldering trays as steam hissed from the kitchen vents. Beyond, supply crews were hauling crates into an airship's belly, their movements practiced and quick. The stronghold carried a rhythm he had come to recognize — order in the noise, purpose in the chaos.

As he cut across the edge of the yard toward the quartermaster's desk, a familiar voice stopped him. He turned and saw her — Ana, standing just outside the mess line, her hands full with a tray. He paused a moment and then removed his helmet and her eyes fixed on him. For a moment, neither spoke.

"I haven't seen you since… before," she said quietly, as though testing whether the sound of her voice would reach him through the armor.

Rich shifted his helmet to under his arm, the black plates across his shoulders catching the morning light. "It's been a while," he said. His voice was steady, but his chest felt heavy with all the words he didn't speak. They had grown close…before.

Her eyes moved over him, taking in the new shape of him. "You've changed," she said finally. "So you're a soldier now."

He nodded once, not trusting more. "Vanguard."

She seemed to search his face for something of the farmer she had known behind the now healed scars of his rebirth. Whatever she looked for, she didn't seem to find it. A silence stretched between them before a voice at the quartermaster's desk barked his name, pulling him away.

"It was good to see you, Ana."

"You too, Rich."

They both knew it was a goodbye. To each other, and to a future that they knew could now never be.

Rich approached the quartermaster's desk. The man looked at him with annoyance for having been caused to wait, but not daring to raise the issue with a vanguard. A stack of orders lay waiting, thin sheets clipped together with his designation scrawled across the top. He stepped forward, helmet tucked under his arm, and accepted the packet.

"Escort detail," the clerk said without looking up. "Convoy runs east. You're with First Squad."

Rich flipped through the pages, skimming past the requisition notes and roster. Standard gear, standard load. His eyes caught on the squad list. Half the names meant nothing to him, but one was circled in his thoughts even as he read past it — a Vanguard he hadn't met before, assigned to the same line. A small-framed Vanguard, whose armor carried a faint yellow cast along the seams, fitted close to her build. The plates didn't make her imposing so much as precise, every movement quick and efficient. Her hair was cropped shorter than most, tucked neatly under the collar, and the rifle resting across her chest looked like an extension of her rather than equipment.

They assembled in the motor yard just after dawn, airships being fueled and loaded in the distance while ground rigs lined up in formation. A sub-commander barked roll call. This wasn't the base commander, but someone who reported to him. His voice carried across the yard, steady and hard-edged, but not the kind that tried too hard to command. This was his squad, and no one questioned it.

Rich took his place among them, armor sealed and humming at his joints. He stood shoulder to shoulder with soldiers he didn't know, the quiet weight of their shared purpose pulling them together. Across the line, he saw the same small-framed Vanguard adjusting the strap of her rifle, her helmet clipped at her side. Their eyes met briefly — just a glance, an acknowledgment — before the sergeant's voice cut across the space again.

"This is a routine run. Diplomatic envoy and supplies. Nothing fancy, nothing unexpected. We deliver them to the outer stronghold; we bring them back. You're Vanguard now. You make sure nothing touches them. Clear?"

A chorus of affirmations rose from the line.

The sergeant scanned their faces, his expression unreadable beneath the morning light. "Mount up."

Engines coughed to life as the convoy began its crawl toward the gates. Rich settled into his place, hands steady on the rails, the weight of the orders still firm in his chest. It was his first mission as a vanguard. Nothing flashy, but satisfaction sat deep in his chest as he felt the convoy exit the gates. He glanced at where his farm would have been. They had moved several times since he had given up that life, but their farm had always been in the same relative place.

He saw a few people working the land. He surveyed their layout, what crops they were growing with mild interest. He pushed the thoughts away before deeper pain of his past life set in and he focused forward on the mission ahead.

Rich left the top of the crawler and settled into a seat inside, leaning his back against a pile of the supplies they were supposed to be bringing to another stronghold for trade.

He found himself again beside the small-framed Vanguard, whose armor bore the faint yellow cast along its seams. She checked her gear, her movements practiced and precise. Her helmet hung from her belt, catching the morning light. She glanced at him, her eyes steady.

She studied him a moment, then asked, "First mission?"

"Yeah," Rich admitted. "Yours?"

"Third," she said, tightening the strap on her rifle. "Still new. Still feels strange."

Rich gave a small grunt. "Guess that makes two of us."

"You're the one that used to be a farmer, right? Took out that raider group and got recruited?"

Rich sat in silence for a minute. He had known a few people heard his story, but didn't expect it to be brought up on a mission.

He nodded.

"Yeah, I'm Rich. What about you? Where did you come from?"

"I'm Grassie, at least that's what they started calling me. Might as well go with it. I was an engineer. Helped process the trexium that came up from the mines." She paused, eyes distant for a moment. "Not the kind of work you expect to lead here. But sometimes you gotta put down a wrench for a rifle, and that can get you noticed. Plus, the food is better. Ever tried matcha?"

Rich shook his head.

"You should, it's the best. We didn't get that kind of food in engineering."

She left it at that, the corners of her mouth tightening as if there was more she would not say. It was enough to mark that her path to Vanguard had been anything but simple.

A faint smile tugged at the corner of her mouth before she grew serious again. "Hey, watch my back out there." Her tone was quiet, almost casual, though the weight of it landed heavy.

Rich hesitated before nodding. "I will. As long as you watch mine."

For a moment, there was a trace of something like understanding between them. But as soon as the words left him, unease pressed at his chest. His mind dragged back to the farm, to

Mita and Hagan, to the fact that when it had mattered most, he hadn't been enough. The thought slid cold through him, even as he tried to bury it. He wondered if she could see the doubt in his eyes.

She gave no sign, only began fiddling with something on her wrist console, changing some setting within her armor and getting dialed in before they arrived.

The airships above the right he sat in shadowed their convoy, engines thrumming steady as they traced the route east. Hours passed in routine silence, the monotony broken only by the grind of treads and the occasional barked order.

When the other stronghold came into view over the ridge, the mountains of the valley that encircled them rising not far beyond. Above them, the storm that kept them all locked in together, unable to travel to the next valley raged, lightning hitting ridges in rhythmic, almost predictable patterns.

Rich studied the walls of the stronghold in the distance, zooming in with a touch of the controls on his wrist. Panels patched with different alloys, guard towers bristling with weapons, the whole structure carrying a posture of wariness. The convoy slowed as they reached the rendezvous point. Caravans never went into other strongholds. Too much danger of deception, of losing all the supplies you offered without gaining anything for yourself. This stronghold had a reputation for taking more than they gave. Soldiers filed forward away from the other stronghold, their uniforms marked by colors Rich didn't recognize. The trade began—crates unloaded, manifests checked, the clatter of supplies changing hands.

Everything was going more smoothly than Rich could have hoped. He stood near the edge of his rig, seeing Grassie on the corner of another crawler with her rifle held low, the pink core playing over the yellow streaks in her armor. Rich caught sight of the envoy officers discussing in calm, assertive tones with his counterpart.

Before he could figure out why, the air changed. Voices sharpened. A command rang out in a language Rich didn't know, and suddenly rifles were rising. The first shot cracked through the aft, striking one of the escorts at the edge of the line. Chaos followed as enemy fire poured from entrenched positions along the ridges near the rendezvous. Figures in unfamiliar uniforms burst from cover, weapons flashing, cutting into the convoy without warning.

Rich dropped into cover, the hum of his armor alive against his skin. Around him the squad scattered, shouting over the din. He looked around at the rest of the vanguard, who fired back and fought with practiced precision. He marveled that he could count himself among them. His mind turned to Grassie. He found her, her small frame pinned behind a supply crate, trexium fire from enemy vanguard chewing the ground around her. She moved to return fire, but a blast from the ridge sent the crate collapsing in shards, knocking her to the ground.

Without thinking, Rich surged forward. His rifle spat bursts at the line of enemy soldiers dug in along the rocks near the rendezvous. He reached her side, hauling her up by the straps of her armor, dragging her clear as another blast scorched the dirt where she had lain. Together they stumbled into the shadow of the crawler, its bulk shielding them for a moment, far enough from the stronghold's walls to avoid their heavier guns.

Rich leaned out from cover, his rifle barking controlled bursts. Each shot struck true, dropping enemy soldiers who thought themselves hidden among the rocks. Years of farm work had built his arms to steady weight; his new training had taught him how to aim it. He cut down one after another, forcing the line to falter. Slowly though, rounds began eating away at the crawler, taking bites out and exposing them to the elements.

"We can't stay here!" Grassie called as she fired back through a new hole in the side of the vehicle.

Rich looked out and found an outcropping of rock that would shield them better.

"There, move, move!" Rich shouted, taking command of the situation.

The two of them burst from the crumbling remains of their failing haven sprinting across the dry earth, dust kicking up behind them, signalling their movements to the enemies firing down at them.

A pink flash lit the walls of the stronghold directly in his eye line. Rich saw the blast coming before she did. He shoved her down and turned, taking the hit of the trexium round across his shoulders and back. The impact staggered him, his armor groaning under the force. Pain lanced through him, but he held his ground. His size and strength absorbed what might have crushed her, his body a shield against the worst of it.

She scrambled back to her feet, eyes wide inside the visor. "You—" she started, but Rich was already firing again, making their attackers take cover and giving them the time needed to continue the run across the open landscape.

Once they were behind the rock, he checked her once more, just long enough to see that she was upright, unhurt. Relief hit sharp in his chest, colliding with grief that never left him. Inside the helmet, tears slipped unseen — for Mita and Hagan, for what he had lost, and for the fierce relief of protecting someone when it mattered. He knew they would come again in every battle to follow. His helmet would hide them, his grief and his redemption, his alone.

Chapter 10 – The War Angels

Rich spent the next years of his life training, protecting, grieving, and working his way up in the ranks of the Vanguard. Eventually he found himself in what he and many considered to be the top squad in the entire Coalition. The five of them ran mission that no other team would even dare take on. Today was one of those days.

Orders spread fast, with almost no time to breathe between hearing and moving. Delta-Echo-Five had gone dark. The squad had gone to get supplies from a fallen stronghold filled with supplies, wounded, and civilians inside—now swallowed by raiders. Flyer packs here down. Anti-air would cut anything in the sky to pieces. That left Skyhammer. A rig-drop straight into the yard, burn packs to catch at the last moment, and the weight of a squad expected to take the area once boots hit dirt.

Rich stood in the airship. Straps were checked as rigs powered. The trexium cores in their armor whined higher, the air sharp with heat and oil. Armor straps were tugged, weapons snapped to harnesses. This wasn't escort duty.

The squad spoke in fragments, voices carrying that edge before the fall. Grassie ran her hands down her rifle twice more than needed, jaw tight. Cab made a noise that might have been a laugh, though there was nothing behind it. Smokey tried a line meant to cut the tension; it fell flat. Daryas kept her eyes on her weapon, her silence louder than all of it. He watched as Smokey knelt with her and closed something in her hand; the two of them shared a bond. One that none of the rest of them ever chose to brush against.

Rich said nothing. He pulled at the buckles across his chest plate, pressed the seal along his helmet, and felt it catch. He let the weight of it sink onto his shoulders. Skyhammer was as close to a suicide run as a soldier could be handed, but the civilians pinned inside Delta-Echo-Five had nothing at all unless this hammer cracked the ground open.

The rig waited, its hull vibrating under the strain of engines caged and angry.

The ramp sealed. The rig lurched, lifting. The engines' hum pressed through Rich's chest, through the rails he gripped, through his teeth. He braced his boots wider, his breath slow inside the helmet. Everything narrowed to steel, to weight, to the truth that this was the path he chose when he gave up the farm.

Then came the cut. Engines silenced. Gravity took hold.

The Skyhammer began.

Weight vanished and then slammed back into Rich's chest as the hull screamed against the air. Harness straps dug into his shoulders, rattling his armor as the rig knifed down through smoke and cloud. Burn packs flared late, hard, the whole cage jolting so sharp his teeth cracked together. Boots hit steel before his breath returned.

The hatch blew open. The world outside was already fire and chaos.

Trexium rounds carved the air, pink streaks tearing into the yard. Raiders had dug themselves deep along barricades and cargo stacks, weapons mounted, waiting for them to fall. The depot's walls loomed beyond, but the fight had already swallowed the outer grounds.

Rich surged down the ramp with the rest of his team, not support, just Vanguard. Daryas took the center lane, Grassie darted left, Cab roared forward like she meant to smash through concrete. Smokey's rifle snapped with sharp precision from the right edge. Rich anchored the opposite side, heavier than the rest, his steps pounding, rifle spitting fire in measured bursts.

A raider rose from behind a crate, muzzle flashing. Rich's shot caught him center, dropping him flat. Another tried to swing a heavy repeater across the lane—Rich cut him down before the barrel could settle. Years of weight behind shovels had steadied his arms; training had given those arms teeth. Each burst landed, each figure dropped. He felt the line hold because he was there.

Explosions shook the ground, dust and smoke rising so thick it blurred the edges of the field. Through it, Rich saw Grassie vault into cover, her movements sharp and clean. Cab's laughter barked across comms as he broke another flank. Smokey's fire threaded through the haze like a needle, each shot carving a path. And at the center, Daryas drove forward, relentless.

Rich shifted with them, holding the right, firing steadily, absorbing the push as the raiders tried to press back. A trexium blast struck near, heat and force staggering him but leaving the line intact. He dug his boots in and fired again, each squeeze of the trigger punching holes in the assault. He was the wall on the flank, and he held.

A secondary blast tore into a cargo stack nearby, sending slabs of steel and concrete shearing loose. The debris crashed down in a spray of dust and sparks, cutting Grassie off and threatening to bury her position. Rich moved without thinking; his size carrying him where others would have been slowed. Armor plates scraped against shattered concrete as he forced his way between the falling wreckage and Grassie, his frame filling the gap like a barricade. The trexium blast that followed would have cut her down—his bulk took the shards across his shoulders and chest, the armor groaning but holding. He braced, absorbed the hit, then lifted his rifle and dropped the raiders who had fired it. Their stolen vanguard weapons, too powerful for them to wield effectively without the reinforced armor, clattered to the ground.

Grassie slid back into position at his side, dust streaking her visor. "Just like old times," she said, voice tight but steady across comms.

Rich gave a short grunt as one of the first tears that always graced him in battle, his silent remembrance of those he cared for and wasn't able to save, fell down his face before snapping another burst into the haze. "Let's make sure there are more of them."

Together they pushed forward, Grassie moving low and quick, striking from cover, Rich rising tall beside her, every step a wall of steel and muscle. His rounds slammed into entrenched raiders, breaking their push. Her shots stitched the gaps he couldn't reach. Protector and striker, side by side, the rhythm of their movements drawing them deeper into the fight.

Cab's bellow rolled across the yard as he broke another flank wide. Daryas's fire drove the center forward, never slowing. The squad pressed, unrelenting. Rich felt the weight of it in his chest— this was what it meant to hold, to stand where others might fall. He absorbed the storm, his strength feeding theirs.

The battle stretched on, fire and smoke thick enough to burn the lungs even through the filters. Rich held his lane, rifle hammering rhythm into the chaos, until the field began to splinter. Cab's roar pulled left as he followed, Grassie slid right trading shots with raiders, and somewhere ahead Daryas's voice crackled once over comms before cutting away—she had broken toward the depot, toward the civilians trapped inside. That left the yard to the rest of them.

Rich pressed forward, boots grinding through rubble. The line buckled, then steadied under his weight. He could feel the fight changing, tension pulling toward a single point ahead. Through the haze he caught sight of Smokey breaking from cover, rifle flashing as he pressed toward a lone figure who didn't move like the rest.

Kallan "One Shot" Brigg.

Across the debris-strewn courtyard, Smokey was locked in brutal hand-to-hand against a broad, scarred figure clad in a patchwork of Coalition armor and scavenged gear. Even at a distance, Rich could see the smile splitting Brigg's face—wide, cruel, hungry for the kill. Smokey moved fast—his blade flashing in tight arcs, dodging brutal swings—but Brigg fought like a bludgeon, smashing him back with sheer mass and feral precision.

Rich tried to cut across, rifle spitting bursts, but raiders spilled into his lane, hemming him in. He dropped them one by one, but the distance to Smokey only grew, the fight pulling further from his reach. Grassie and Cab were pinned at their own angles, too far to intervene. Through the haze, Rich glimpsed Smokey slam hard into a pile of broken crates, his knife torn from his hand, blood streaking his face.

Brigg's grin widened. He drew a machete slow, almost lovingly, the edge glinting red against the smoke. His voice carried even through the chaos: "I've heard about you. Best shot in the Vanguard, they say."

Smokey spat blood into the dust but didn't answer. Brigg pressed the flat of the blade against Smokey's cheek, tilting his head roughly to the side. "Let's see how sharp that eye really is."

Rich roared, cutting down raiders that barred his way, but he was still too far. He could see it clearly: Smokey pinned, Brigg crouched above, blade poised for the kill, slicing slowly into Smokey's face. For all Rich's size, for all his strength, he was too slow; he was going to fail again.

Thoughts of Mita and Hagan racked his mind, and he replayed his grief and horror at failing to protect those he loved, and here was Smokey, too far to be saved.

Then another shot cracked, not Brigg's. A blast bright enough to sear through the haze, powered by a core that burned hotter than issue. Daryas's rifle roared from a ridge to his left, the shot tearing through Brigg's temple and dropping him mid-execution. The raider hit the ground hard, machete clattering free.

The yard staggered into silence, broken only by the hiss of burning trexium and the groans of the wounded. Smokey slumped to his knees, one hand pressed against the side of his bloodied face, but alive. Across the yard stood Daryas, rifle still raised, chest heaving with the effort of the shot. She had returned from the depot, civilians safe behind her.

Rich lowered his weapon slowly, breath raw inside the helmet. He had seen Smokey's life about to be taken, and for all his size, for all his strength, he hadn't been able to close the gap. The kill had come from Daryas, impossible and absolute. Relief surged, but so did the old grief. His tears burned hot as they slid down his cheeks, hidden by black steel.

Delta-Echo-Five loomed behind them in the dying light, smoke rising from the broken walls like the last breath of something too stubborn to fall cleanly. The civilians were huddled in small groups near the medical rigs—shaken, bleeding, but alive. Their eyes slid toward the squad and away again, unsure whether to see them as saviors or something harsher.

Daryas stood with her rifle slung across her chest, her armor scorched and cracked along the forearms and thighs where the landing had bitten hardest. She carried herself like she didn't feel it. Not yet.

The squad pulled into a loose half-circle near the loading ramp. Grassie wiped blood and dust from her faceplate, helmet tucked under her arm, her braid half-torn and hanging. Cab lowered herself onto a crate, nose split and bleeding, her helmet dangling from tired fingers. Smokey lingered in the shadow of the rig's frame, stitches raw across his face, one eye swollen shut, the other fixed on Daryas with something that passed between them unspoken.

Rich leaned against the rig wall, arms folded, rifle resting across his chest. The helmet stayed on. He didn't want them to see what was still wet on his face. Watching was easier than speaking.

The crunch of boots cut through the quiet. Commander Hartwell strode into view, armor still dusted white with ash from the courtyard fires. He stopped in front of them, helmet tucked beneath one arm, his gaze heavy.

"You pulled them out," he said at last, voice rough from smoke. "All of them."

His eyes flicked toward the civilians, then back. "You hit that yard like an airstrike. Fast. Brutal." He shook his head once. "Like an air strike from heaven."

The words carried more weight than Rich expected. He felt them settle into the silence, heavier than any praise. Hartwell turned and walked away, shouting orders to the med teams.

No one in the squad moved. No one spoke. The air hung thick with exhaustion and everything they'd just survived.

Daryas tugged the strap of her rifle tight, her hand brushing the battered, spent core at her hip. Smokey caught her eye and gave the smallest nod. She returned it, steady, certain.

Rich shifted against the wall, feeling the ache of his muscles, the sting beneath the armor, and the burn of tears that hadn't dried. No one would ever see them. That was his vow. Grief stayed his, hidden behind black plates, even as the name Hartwell had given them echoed in his chest.

They had fallen like a hammer from heaven. Not soldiers, not farmers, not survivors anymore—something else. Angels forged for a single purpose.

They were the War Angels.

Around The Fire

The chill on the ridge between the slabs of stone settled deeper into the air as Rich's voice fell quiet.

He hadn't rushed it, hadn't dressed it up—just put the story down, steady and plain, the way he carried most things. For a long moment, nobody spoke. The fire cracked and hissed, smoke slipping into the night.

Cab flicked a pebble into the flames, causing a stream of sparks to spiral into the sky. "Damn," she muttered. "Guess that's why you never laugh at my jokes."

Rich's mouth twitched, almost a smile. "No. That's not why. They're just not funny."

Grassie chuckled, low and rough. "Finally, someone says it."

Cab pointed across the fire. "Traitor."

Miner hid a smirk behind his mug. This was the rhythm of them—breaking weight with banter before it pinned anyone too deep.

Daryas didn't let it drift long. She leaned forward, elbows on her knees, eyes still on Rich. "You carried that a long time."

"Long enough," Rich said flatly.

Grassie's knife clicked softly against her boot. "Could still be out there, you know? Kids find ways to slip through cracks."

Rich's eyes lifted, flat and hard. "No."

Cab sat forward. "But you don't know that—"

"Cab," Daryas cut in, voice sharp enough to stop her.

Rich didn't let the silence land before he finished it himself. "If I let that stand in me, I'd never stop. I'd burn everything I've got chasing what's already gone. Not doing that."

No one pressed again. Cab shifted the pebble in her hand but didn't throw it. Grassie leaned back, braid sliding further loose. Miner tipped his mug, stared into the coals.

The fire popped, and for a while that was the only sound.

Then Cab huffed, shaking her head. "Still can't believe we're sitting here. You remember Haven Ridge?"

Daryas groaned. "Don't start."

"No, come on. Haven Ridge." Cab laughed at herself, shoulders shaking. "Three squads stacked into one crawler. Half the wheels blown before we even hit the hill. Rich trying to push the damn thing uphill with his shoulders—"

Grassie barked another laugh. "And you yelling at him to keep it steady while you were sliding off the back."

Cab pointed with the pebble she still hadn't tossed. "Don't act like you weren't hanging on my armor, screaming louder than I was."

Daryas actually chuckled at that, quiet but genuine. "That ridge nearly killed all of us."

"Yeah," Cab said, grinning despite herself. "But we made it."

Grassie's grin was smaller, more tired. "Barely."

Rich shook his head, but the corner of his mouth betrayed him again. "Barely still counts."

The fire flared as a gust rolled over the ridge, sparks lifting toward the stars before dropping back to ash.

Grassie turned her knife once more in her palm, then set it flat across her boot. She leaned back, exhaled through her nose. "Alright. Guess it's my turn."

Cab perked up instantly. "Oh, this'll be good."

Grassie shot her a look. "It's not a show."

"Could've fooled me." Cab tossed the pebble at last, and it hissed into the flames.

"Cab," Daryas said again, though this time it carried no edge.

Miner's smirk tugged back into place.

Grassie stretched her legs out, got comfortable against the stone. She stared at the fire a long beat, allowing the flames to dance over the yellow streaks in her armor, then lifted her eyes to the rest of them.

"Alright," she said. "Where to start?"